EMOTIONALLY SILENT:

Transitioning Through An Imperfect Journey

the memoir of
Samgrelletta Z. Fairley

S. Z. FAIRLEY ENTERPRISES LLC
Washington, DC

This book is dedicated to my father James Fairley who was always there for me, supporting me, protecting me and providing for me. Just hearing his voice would always make things better.

Table of Contents

CHAPTER 1   **11**
Early life

CHAPTER 2   **17**
Pre-teen Life

CHAPTER 3   **27**
Teenage Life

CHAPTER 4   **33**
Welcome to Atlanta

CHAPTER 5   **43**
Military/Transitional Life

CHAPTER 6   **61**
Rape

CHAPTER 7   **65**
Life After Military

CHAPTER 8   **71**
First Job/First Relationship

CHAPTER 9   **81**
Deputy Sheriff

CHAPTER 10   **95**
From Relationship to Jail

CHAPTER 11   **113**
Georgia Regional

CHAPTER 12   **127**
Out of Control

CHAPTER 13   **137**
Precious and Champ

CHAPTER 14   **151**
New York

CHAPTER 15   **165**
Wrong is Wrong

CHAPTER 16   **181**
Megan My Friend

CHAPTER 17   **191**
My Future

CHAPTER 18   **217**
My Hero Is Gone

CHAPTER 19   **225**
Mr. Chico

CHAPTER 20   **229**
Mental Health

INTRODUCTION

To a lesbian, being one is something to be proud of because you are expressing who you are. Being a lesbian also means being in the closet for fear of rejection in today's society. For most of my life I had to live my life emotionally silent.

Many times, I had found myself hiding from myself. I would often question God. I've asked him why he allowed me to go through certain situations in my life? Why did he not help me speak up? What happened to my voice and why was I afraid to identify with my true self?

In "Emotionally Silent," I share my story of molestation, racism, lesbianism, depression, being arrested, P.T.S.D, domestic violence and lupus. As a child who grew up Catholic and a tomboy, I always tried to be a little girl who did all the things a little girl should do. I tried to be that little girl for my parents, especially for my mother. This book follows my life as I saw it. It took me over two decades to come to the realization that I did not have to be or live emotionally silent anymore. I did not have to keep hurting and being unhappy while I made sure everyone else around me was happy. Once I spoke up I began to live with the person I had become and without fear of rejection or being judged. If I had known how to communicate growing up then maybe I would not have allowed myself to go through the hurt I endured. Instead, I allowed all these things to affect my mental health as I got older.

As you read this book, please understand it is written through my eyes only. You will see the before of who I am and the price I paid to get to who I have become.

CHAPTER 1

Early Life

I was born in my mothers' bedroom in 1966 in a small town in rural Mississippi, weighing 5lbs, 2 oz. We lived in a farming area. When my mother found out she was pregnant, my dad was just drafted into the US Army and would be gone for the next two years.

At five months I was diagnosed with a club foot at the Laurel, MS Health Clinic. This meant that my foot was curved inside which made it difficult for me to walk with my foot flat on the ground. It would be as if I was walking on the outside edges of my foot, so I was fitted with special shoes mounted on a bar which I wore for about 14 months.

When I turned 18 months old, my dad returned home from the Army. This was his first time seeing me. He spent a few weeks with me and then travelled to Chicago to seek employment. During this time, 1968, the north was the place to go for work. Shortly afterwards, my mom prepared to join my dad in Chicago.

My dad worked two jobs most of the time. We lived in a flat on Central Park and Madison Street in Chicago, Illinois. Six months later, we moved to an apartment on Lake Street and Latrobe. My room consisted of a roll-a-way bed in the dining room next to my pet turtle and two birds. I was alright not having my own room but I had one problem with my room being in the dining room. There was a big rat that would roam around at night that my dad couldn't catch. He would use the biggest traps he could find. I also did not like the fact that my parents would close their bedroom door at night and leave me in the dining room with the rat. I think I woke up sweaty every morning from sleeping with my head covered up for fear that the rat might bite me in my face. It took a while but one day my dad finally caught it. It was huge. To a person my size it looked as big as a cat.

My parents only had one car so I would watch my mother catch a cab to work and then my dad and I would pick her up that evening. Growing up in Chicago was good. I can remember during the cold winters I used to play on the heater that looked like an accordion. Being an only child, I had to amuse myself but I found out there were a lot of perks. For Christmas I pretty much got everything I wanted on my list. My mom bought me all kinds of dolls, including a life-sized one that I named Wilomina. I also had a Barbie doll house with furniture and accessories. I did want a sibling but unknown to me at the time, my mother was not able to have any more children and I think God had a plan with that because my future gave my mother a run for her money.

Three or four years old was the age for me to start going to daycare. I remember it being in a gym because we rode on Big Wheels and took naps on floor mats and drank a small glass of milk with one cookie. During this time we lived on Lake Street until we were able to move around the corner to North Latrobe in a 2nd floor flat. I really thought we had moved on up like The Jefferson's.

Even though I was very young, I had a crush on the landlord. She and her husband lived on the first floor. I did not like him much because he was abusive toward her but that was none of my business. The landlord's husband had a teenage daughter who would visit. One time during a visit her parents were not at home. I don't remember if she was babysitting me that day or if I was just there for a play-date. I noticed that she always liked to play Hide and Seek with me. When we would play, for some reason I would always hide behind a bed and she would find me. It was what she did after she found me that changed the course of my innocence. Once she found me, she would play touchy feely and ask me for a kiss. I did not realize she was doing something wrong. I thought it was part of the game.

Meanwhile, both my parents worked during the day so I would go to a babysitter across the alley from our two flats. This was actually the same building we moved from. The babysitter was a nice lady who lived with two of her sisters. She also had a brother, but he did not live with them.

On several occasions her brother would come by and visit with my babysitter. After time went on, the visits from her brother became more frequent. He began playing with me more often because my babysitter watched TV a lot. On one particular day, I wanted to lay down so my babysitter told me to go in her room and lay down. Shortly afterward, I am not sure if my babysitter fell asleep but her brother came in the room with me. She had no idea that her brother had started molesting me. It started out with him having me rub on his private parts. After more visits it got to the point where he would make me do things no child should do with an adult. I was scared to tell. Besides, he said nothing was wrong with what he was doing. I remained emotionally silent and never told my mother until almost 40 years later. The reason I remained silent was because I was afraid of my mom. I was afraid to talk to her about things that mother/daughter should be able to talk about. I think I was always afraid of getting in trouble so I remained emotionally silent.

After those ordeals, it was time for me to start school so I no longer needed a babysitter. I started 1st grade at St. Thomas Aquinas in Chicago, Illinois and continued my education there through 2nd grade. My Mom would drop me off on her way to work each day. I don't remember much about my 1st grade year, but I do remember 2nd grade; I had my first so-called boyfriend that year. His name was George. He was very cute and had the most gorgeous dimples. After I completed my 2nd grade year, my family moved into our first home in Maywood, Illinois in 1974. We had made it to the suburbs.

CHAPTER 2

Pre-Teen Life

While in Maywood I remember living next door to an elderly woman who my mom befriended and started helping by taking her to the store or helping her with whatever she needed help with. One day my mom took our neighbor to a store called Zayre. Before we left for the store, my mom had already told me she was not buying me anything and don't ask for anything. After we got to the store I saw some crayons I wanted. I asked my mom anyway and naturally she told me she was not going to buy them. While she was shopping with our neighbor I walked away from her. I went back to the crayons, picked them up and put them in my pocket. I also saw some zebra striped gum and put that in my pocket as well. Oh, my God, what did I do that for?

On our way back from the store I could not wait to eat a piece of gum. I thought my mom was preoccupied with talking with our neighbor which meant that she was not paying attention to me. I reached into my pocket, got a piece of gum, bent my head over and stuck it in my mouth. I was sitting in the back seat just chewing away. Unbeknownst to me, there was a such thing called a rear-view mirror. By the time we got home I spit the gum out when my mom was letting our neighbor out of the car. When we got in the house, my mom asked me for the gum. I said, "what gum". She said, "the gum you were chewing that I did not buy". I gave her the gum and then she asked me if I had anything else. I reached in my pocket and gave her the crayons. I don't remember a butt whooping but I do remember crying all the way back to the store. My mom had taken me back to the store and made me tell the manager what I did and then returned the items I stole. Never again did I steal.

While living in Maywood, my mom started letting me spend my summers in Mississippi. On my first trip, my cousins thought I was dumb because I didn't know the difference between a chicken and a turkey. I was a city girl, not a country girl. After a lesson from my grandad, I quickly learned the difference.

I would spend my summers between my Aunt Mavis, my Grandma Elizabeth and my Grandma Corene. When I would stay with my aunt, I would always get into trouble with my cousin, Justin. When I would stay with my Grandma Elizabeth, I would be there with my other cousins. I had a lot of fun because there would be about five or six of us and all of us would sleep in one bed but we did not mind. During the day Grandma would make each one of us a tea cake and then go to work. She lived in a wooded area on a hill in a pink house. She did not have a bathroom nor did she have running water. She had well water. If we had to use the bathroom we went it the woods or we used her outhouse. I was afraid to go in the outhouse because I was scared I was going to fall in the hole. If we did not have toilet paper, we would use leaves. Believe it or not, I would rather stay with Grandma Elizabeth than with my Grandma Corene, who did have a bathroom and running water—and washer and dryer.

When I would visit my grandma Corene, I would help her on their farm. Our dinner was what she grew on the farm. Grandma also worked at the local chicken plant and that would be our meat. We picked butterbeans, peas, okra, potatoes, corn and watermelon. I loved shelling peas because I liked shooting them at my uncle Barry and sometimes Justin and his brothers would be there. Barry was very spoiled, and he was only a few years older than me. Every summer he would terrorize all of us but we knew he loved us in his own way. When my grandparents were not working they drank Budweiser and played spades with family and friends. When they did that I knew we would be skipping our bath time. Most of the time my uncle and I would take a bath together to save water. That is until I learned his body parts were different than mine and grandma stopped that immediately. Half the time we did not take a real bath anyway. Just like any other kid we would splash the water around and make it sound like we were bathing. After another one of my summer trips to Mississippi, I returned home and had picked up my uncle Barry's southern accent. I sounded so much like my uncle, if you were not looking at me you would have thought it was him talking. After about a week back home, I lost the accent because momma didn't play that .

By now, I was around nine or ten years old. I was attending St. Eulalia Elementary School. I attended this school through the 8th grade. The school was taught by nuns, but they did not wear the stereotypical outfits. I was a good student but I was also the class clown most of the time. I had two boyfriends, Pierre and Vincent. There were other boys who liked me but I did not like them. I never really did anything physical with them; we just called ourselves boyfriend and girlfriend. Pierre was who I liked the most. He was a star football player for the school and he was the first boy I kissed.

Maywood was a very nice community. The parents knew all the kids on the block and would call a parent if we got out of line. Between my Godparents (R. E. and Joan) and the Guthrie family (next door neighbors), they were able to help with my after-school care while my parents worked. Often when I got out of school, I would have to stay with the Guthrie's until my mom got home from work. My neighbor had a son named Troy. I considered him my big brother because he kind of looked after me like I was his little sister.

In our community the boys outnumbered the girls. I was a tomboy in the neighborhood. I had many friends on my block and many of them were already in high school. Even though I was young, I tried to hang out with them but I also hung out with kids my age. We were one big happy neighborhood. After about a year my parents started letting me stay at home by myself. Then a year after that my mom started letting me go outside while she was at work since it would get dark before she got home from work. The only thing I had to do was go straight home after school and call her. The school was less than a block from the house so she knew around what time I should have been calling her every day. I was also supposed to call her every hour while I was outside.

One day I did not go straight home. I think I was playing around after school and forgot to call my mom when I finally got home. After I got home, my best friend Julianna's boyfriend Chris came over with his dog Petey. Now I was not supposed to have company when no one was home but my dumb butt decided to let Chris in the house. Chris came in and we went up to my room. I had no hidden agenda and besides he was Julianna's boyfriend.

During this time both my parents smoked cigarettes and they kept boxes of matches in a kitchen drawer. I don't know what gave me the idea of playing with matches in my room and throwing them out my bedroom window. My window faced the street. Chris and I just started striking matches and throwing them out of the window. After Chris and I struck all the matches I went downstairs to get some more. When I got back upstairs I looked out the window and saw my mom's car. Now remember, I never called my mom to let her know I was home. Unbeknownst to me, one of the neighbors called my mom at work to let her know Chris and I were throwing matches from my upstairs bedroom window. My mom had caught me in the act. I freaked out. I heard my mom come in the house so I pushed Chris and his dog in my bedroom closet. I told him not to make any noise and then I went downstairs and tried to dumped the matches in the garbage in some water. My mom came in and said, "What's burning?" My stupid butt said, "I don't know," but she had already noticed I was in the upstairs window. Lord, when she walked up in my room Chris was standing in the middle of my bedroom holding his dog. All I remember was that Chris jumped down all 12 steps and ran out the front door. Meanwhile, I got my butt whipped. While my mom was whipping me, I decided to run from her around our dining room table. What did I do that for? My mom turned into Annie Oakley and that belt turned into a lasso. She swung that lasso and I did not duck in time. The belt buckle caught me in my face. When I went back to school the next day I just told him I got into trouble. Little did he know the scar on my face was from that butt whipping. That was the last time I had company and played with matches. I still have a scar to this day.

I always got into trouble with my mom because I was always lying about something. I think I got a daily butt whipping. I also think I got pre-whippings. I think I got a whipping for something I might do the next day.

A couple of months later my parents bought me a dog. I guess they felt this would give me something to do and keep me out of trouble. We named him Shannon. He was a black Poodle/Cocker Spaniel mix. I had something I was now responsible for.

Even though I had Shannon, I would still go to Mississippi during the summers. A majority of my visits were with my grandma Corene. Still a tomboy, I started having crushes on my uncle's girlfriends. I could not figure out my feelings or figure out why I was attracted to women. I knew that it was not normal so I felt that I was not normal so I stayed emotionally silent.

Meanwhile, uncle Barry would always get us in trouble with my grandma. Especially when Justin and his brothers, Erick and Jacob would come over. He was always throwing things at us like cucumbers and potatoes from my grandma's farm. One day he chased us in the house and we went to hide from him. Jacob, the youngest, and I hid under one of the beds that was up against a wall. We thought we were back far enough so that he could not see us but we were not. I hid behind Jacob so I was up against the wall. We did not know that uncle Barry was going to throw a Vicks vapor rub bottle under the bed. It hit Jacob in the forehead, and we all got in trouble because it left a knot on his head.

Another incident was when Uncle Barry made his horse throw me off of it and I landed on the carport on my shoulder. He kept us in trouble. Some days he would have us walk barefooted to town just to go to the store or over an aunt's house. Back then it did not seem that far. Now that I think about, that was about a six-mile walk.

Uncle Barry was about 9 or 10 years old when learned

how to drive but we could never use the car to go to town. However, with my grandparents being beer drinkers they would send us to the neighboring town to get them beer. The neighboring town was about 9 miles away. Barry would get a pillow and sit on it while he drove to the store because he was kind of short and I was right there in the car with him. That was how I enjoyed my summers with my family.

Growing up, I really don't remember having too many mother-daughter conversations between me and my mom. What I do remember is the talk about my menstrual cycle. When I was eleven years old, I woke up one morning for school because it happened. I told my mom and she had to be late to work because she had to go to the store and get me some maxi pads.

As a student, my parents had a couple of parent-teacher conferences. Most of the time it was about my conduct. I was an average student. I was not a student who would fight; I was the type of student to break them up. The only so-called fight I had was with a boy named Tom. I don't remember why but I do know I punched him in his nose. I was being egged on by other students, although I did not really want to hit him. I apologized to him the next day.

I had a birthday roll around and my parents bought me a brand new 10-speed bike from Sears department store. This was after I took my pink banana seat bike to

Mississippi for a summer and my uncle Barry sold it for parts. Unfortunately, it was not too long before someone stole my 10-speed out of the back yard. I never got another bike. For the next few years, I was a typical teenager getting into trouble and trying to lie my way out of it. I was really working my mother's nerves. At one point she mentioned sending me to boarding school but my dad would not let her. I don't really know if she meant it but I guess that was how bad I was.

CHAPTER 3

Teenage Life

By the time I was in the eighth grade, my mother introduced me to her best friend and co-worker, Jen. They played on the same company softball team. I ended up meeting her son Reginald who would visit from Indiana for the summers. He ended up being my boyfriend. I was 13 and he was 16. We would get together anytime our folks got together. It was more so puppy love for me. He was very cute. He taught me how to kiss. It was my first French kiss. It was kind of awkward because I was used to the T.V. kisses with just lip to lip. During my first try, I ended up with my mouth just sitting inside of his. I was just sitting there not knowing what the hell I was doing. Then he taught me the 411 on kissing. I was swapping spit. It was different.

While in the eighth grade my parents and I decided it was time for me to get baptized. Unfortunately, I had asked my favorite teacher to be my godmother and my parents asked our neighbors R. E. and Joan, so all of them were there. I was baptized a Catholic. It was the right thing to do since I had been attending Catholic schools and churches for so long.

My last year of school, I tried out for the cheerleading team. That was only because I think my mom got tired of me being a tomboy. I like sports but I think my mother wanted a prissy little girl but that was not me. Anyway, I tried out for the squad and ended up making it. Mom was very proud of me. It made her happy.

During this time, I was still seeing Reginald. One day he and a friend came to one of my cheerleading practices. He started acting funny for no reason. I think he wanted to go to the next stage of the relationship.......Sex. I was very scared. I knew I did not want to have sex with him or any other boy. I was not into that at all, especially at the age of 13. Later our relationship dissolved. He went back to Indiana and I went about my business. Later, eighth grade graduation came around. After graduation, Reginald expressed to me that he wanted to get back together. We did but with a better understanding. We had started talking about how many kids we were going to have together even though he was still living in Indiana. This was also soon to be my first year in high school.

Before high school began, my parents and I went to visit my Aunt Colette and her family and Aunt Gladys in Atlanta. They were Grandma Elizabeth sisters. At the time, I had no idea we were going to be moving to Atlanta shortly afterwards. When we returned from our trip, it was time for me to start high school. My parents again wanted me to go to the best school so they sent me to an all-girl Christian school (Immaculate Heart of Mary) in Westchester, Illinois. It was across the street from the all-boy school (St Joseph). My new school had to wear uniforms. A couple of my friends that graduated from St Eulalia were also going there so I knew I would not be alone. I can remember the first day. My mother had to drive me to the school bus stop because it was not within walking distance from our house. I remember sitting in the car crying because I was scared and nervous but I quickly dried my tears when the bus pulled up.

The first day was cool. I could tell there were a lot of prejudice girls at the school but I tried not to be bothered with anyone other than freshman students. You could tell what grade we were in because the uniforms represented each grade with a different color. At some point my mother asked the school if they could add a bus stop. They agreed to do that so that I could be within walking distance. On my bus there was another Black female who was a sophomore. She was very quiet but I sat with her because of the prejudice white students from my school and St. Joseph. Me and the other Black female rode in the front of the bus. One time on the way home the white students were taunting me. When I got off the bus this particular day the students began throwing spit balls at me and they were calling me a "nigger". That was one of the worse days of my life. I thought those days of racism were over. I went home and told my mother. I think the only reason they did not bother the other Black female was because she was a sophomore. My mother went to the school and they reprimanded the students. Needless to say, they did not bother me anymore but I was still scared to ride the bus and so I remained emotionally silent.

About a few weeks later, I asked my mom if I could try out for the basketball team and she said yes. Although I made it, I was not that good. I think they needed a Black female on the team and that was how I was chosen. Being on the team meant that I had to keep my grades up according to my mom and the coach in order to play. My mom even bought me some blue Chuck Taylor All-stars (high top) to play in. After one of our practices, me and some more students were hanging out in the cafeteria. Some of the boys from our brother school came over. This day I noticed a cute boy who looked familiar. His name was

George. Oh my God. It was my second-grade boyfriend from my elementary school. I had not seen him since the 2nd grade. I had to bring my class picture the next day to prove to him that he was my so-called boyfriend. However, he had no interest in me which was okay. I just wanted to play sports anyway. Our team did not win many games but I at least got a letterman's jacket out of it.

About a month into my freshman year, one of my dad's brothers and his family came to visit from Oklahoma. One evening we were all sitting at the dinner table eating dinner when the phone rang. I answered it. The lady on the other end asked to speak to my dad. I thought it was a lady calling him about a job because he was looking for a transfer to Atlanta. It ended up being one of my cousins. I gave the phone to my dad. Then suddenly he sighed and put his hand on his forehead. My mom asked him what was wrong and he said his brother G. B. was killed. My mom grabbed the phone and got more information. I was shocked because I was just begging my uncle for some money a month earlier when I was in Mississippi on summer break. I just went upstairs to my room and sat on my bed and cried. Because of the type of man my dad was he came up to my room, sat on the bed and held me. We were told that my uncle was killed in a construction accident when some heavy machinery fell on him. We all got ready to go to Mississippi for his funeral and afterwards everyone went their separate ways. We returned to Maywood and waited again for word of my dad's transfer.

Dad's transfer finally came just before Christmas. He left before us because my mom still had to wait on her transfer from Illinois Bell. When my mom and I did move, my Uncle Bodie came from Mississippi and helped us move to Atlanta. Meanwhile Reginald did not know we were moving. It happened suddenly. I also did not know he was moving back to Chicago to finish high school and to be with me, but it was too late. My last few days at school, the basketball team gave me a small party, then I left all my friends and headed to another new school. Before leaving, they let me play in my last game. I also got to be in the school newspaper shooting a free throw. It was sad to leave, but I had no choice.

CHAPTER 4

Welcome to Atlanta

When we got to Atlanta we stayed with my Aunt Gladys and Uncle Johnny. My parents found a Christian school for me to complete the second half of my 9th grade year. The school was called Pathway Christian in East Point, Georgia. It was very small. There was only a total of four 9th graders in my class and I was the only Black. I participated in playing the bells while I was there. I knew how to read music considering I played the piano briefly and had started playing the clarinet. It was a nice school. This was also my transformation to a new hair style, the Jherri curl. I also started noticing the language was a little different in the south. It was difficult to transition from saying "pop" to saying "soda" or "drank". Atlanta thought I was backwards. I thought Atlanta was backwards.

My aunt was a housewife and my uncle worked. In her spare time, my aunt babysat for a lady named Ana. Ana had two daughters. I believe I had a crush on Ana even at the age of 14 but I stayed emotionally silent about it. In later years, Ana started taking care of my aunt and uncle as they got older. After about 6 months of living with my aunt, my dad moved us into an apartment in College Park, Georgia for a few months. This was around the time of the Atlanta Missing and Murder Children's investigation. My mother did not let me go anywhere. We lived here for about three months. We had finally found a house in East Point, Georgia. I thought we were rich after seeing the house. It was white with four columns in front of it and it sat on a hill. It was called a tri-level. I only lived there for 3 years. Once we moved into the house, I had to change high schools because the local public high school was closer to our new home. This was the start of my 10th grade year and I went to Lakeshore High School in College Park, Georgia. It was my first time going to a public school.

Before I started my new high school, I let my dad cut my hair but he cut it like a boy. I may have been a tomboy but I really did not want my hair cut like a boy. I knew I did not want to wear dresses and I did not want to show my figure but I was still trying to be my parents' daughter.

At my new school, I joined the band and the chorus in my sophomore year. I joined the basketball team in my junior year. The coach did not let me play much but I enjoyed being on the team. I can at least say that I was the best free throw shooter on the team but the coach still had her favorite players. One player was a lesbian named Clara. After I joined the team, I started hanging with certain people (lesbians) at the school. I did not really have any boyfriends at the school; just wasn't interested. I remember one day getting stopped in the locker room after basketball practice by Clara. She came to my locker and kissed me. I really did not know how to react but a kiss was all it was.

With my dad working at night, he really did not know what was going on with me during my school years. He was always focused on providing for his family. I did not discuss a lot of things with my parents because I did not know how to communicate with them. Me being silly or joking all the time was my way of communicating. I did not want to be an embarrassment to them so I just went to school and played sports while keeping my issues hidden inside and staying emotionally silent.

One day Clara needed a ride to our game. I asked my dad to pick her up. After all she was the star player on the team. What my dad did not know was that his daughter kissed the girl he was picking up. I just wanted to make sure we had our best player at the game. Later on, he found out that Clara was a lesbian. I am not too sure how he found out but he was not too thrilled about it. He never found out about the kiss though. I had a few experiences with females in high school but nothing sexual. The first experience was with a confused 8th grader who thought she wanted to be with a woman. I remember going to her house when her mom was not home and we sat and talked. Then when it was time for me to go, she became a little aggressive. She was trying to lay her head on my shoulder. She wanted a kiss from me before I left so I kissed her, only a peck though. But nothing happened after that. In my junior year I briefly got involved with a 9th grader. I used to go see her a lot when I was supposed to be seeing my best friend who lived across the street from her.

My high school years were good. I was not really interested in guys. I had guys like me, but I did not like them. You know the routine, the ones that like you, you don't like and the ones you like don't like you. By my senior year I started going on dates with guys. I dated one guy from my church. He would come over to my house and all he wanted me to do was rub on his private part. He was a track star who later went on to West Point Military Academy. I also dated this guy from Georgia Tech football team. His sister went to my high school. I dated a guy named Cedric who was an all-American basketball player. He eventually got drafted in 1986 by the Atlanta Hawks but got cut after the first year. I also dated a high school football player from Tucker High School whose cousin dated my cousin Sharon. He was also a star football player for Mississippi State. My mom pretty much liked the guys I chose to date. I think she just liked the fact that I was dating guys. But I never had sex with any of them. I was not into that. Most of the time I hung out with my cousin Sharon a lot. We were the same age and she was like the sister I never had. We would always do the roller-skating thing on the weekends. Once we got our drivers' license, she would get her dads car and we would hang out more.

In 1983, my good friend helped me get my first job at Morrison cafeteria in Hapeville Georgia cleaning up tables. I bussed tables for $2.20 an hour plus tips. By my Senior year, my parents got me a car (1968 Buick Skylark). I loved that car. It had bucket seats and an AM radio with push buttons. I guess they got tired of taking me to work and picking me up from practices. This was also a good way for me and Sharon to get around more. The restaurant was near the Atlanta Airport and I remember seeing professional wrestlers come in and eat together the day after they just beat each other up. I can also remember cleaning the table of Gladys Knight and the Pips minus Gladys. They tipped me three dollars and I asked them to sign each one. I believe my mom still has those dollars.

One day a friend of mine gave me a marijuana cigarette

at school that I had kept in one of my dresser drawers because I did not know how to smoke it. On one of our skating weekends, Sharon, and two of my friends hung out. This is when I learned how to smoke the marijuana cigarette. We were also able to get some beer (private stock) that night also. I was so high I could not drive; Sharon had to. When Sharon and I got back to my house, my parents were still awake. I was so messed up. My eyes were so red. Sharon had to help me keep my composure. I just told my parents I was tired and sleepy. Then I had to go up a flight of stairs. I think Sharon laughed at me the whole time while I was trying to get up the stairs. Oh, my goodness. I think Sharon and I fell asleep in the same bed even though there was a spare bedroom. Then my mom woke us up early making us get up to eat breakfast. This was just how close Sharon and I were. We never missed a weekend of skating. We were either at Golden Glide Skating Rink in Decatur or Skate Towne in College Park, Georgia.

One day at the skating rink I met another lesbian from one of our neighboring high schools and we exchanged numbers. I knew her because we played basketball against each other. She went to Campbell High School in Fairburn Georgia. One night, I got busted talking to her on the telephone because I did not realize my mother was listening on the other end. She was always nosey like that. I can't remember what we were talking about but I am sure it was not a conversation two girls should have been having.

My mother and I had our issues during my high school years, just normal mother daughter situations. She had a habit of going through my things. I did not like that. But she always found what she was looking for. We were not as close as I would have liked to have been during my teenage years. My dad knew we sometimes did not get along and he would try to keep the peace.

My mother was not really at home a lot. She had been going to school and working. Then my dad was working nights, so I hardly saw him. When I did see him he would try to help me with my homework and I appreciated him so much. Even though my dad worked a lot to provide for us, I was his little girl no matter how old I was. I knew just how much he loved me even if we did not spend a lot of time together.

I had a lot of school activities that kept me busy but I really enjoyed being in the band. After one of our football games, a bunch of the band members would hang out on Old National Hwy at the local Pizza Hut. I was also still hanging out with the 9th grader. I remember driving my car to Pizza Hut and cutting my hand on my gear shift. It was bleeding pretty badly. The 9th grader followed me into the restroom and nursed it. She also gave me a kiss until someone came in. At the time I had a so-called girlfriend named Demetrius even though she had a boyfriend. After they broke up, I ended up going to the prom with her ex-boyfriend but it was on a friendly basis. Demetrius and I were never intimate. We would only kiss every now and then because I really did not know what else to do. I think my mom knew about us but she never said anything and I never admitted anything.

I very rarely missed any days of school. The only time I missed school was if we were out of town. I was never suspended until Senior skip day. All the seniors who could get a car drove around the school like a parade just blowing the car horns. Luckily I got my moms' approval prior and she knew about it before the principal called her. With my mom being an active parent, the principal knew who I was right away. It was all in fun.

Before my senior year started, my parents let me get another job at Taco Bell. It was fun working and making my own money. After my summer job was over, that school year was filled with band practice, basketball practice and classes. When it was time for me to get ready for graduation I almost did not graduate. I had to take two English classes in my last semester and I was not a good English student at all. I was praying I passed because I had family members coming to my graduation. I was going to be the first grandchild to graduate high school. Luckily I was able to graduate by getting two D's out of both classes. My next move was to go to college. I wanted to be like my Aunt Sandie from Detroit who studied nursing and was in the Army Reserve. I started applying to these big-name schools, not knowing my grades were not going to get me in. I think my GPA was (1.0). I could not apply for financial aid because my parents made too much money at the time. I did get accepted to Clayton Junior College in Morrow, Georgia. I also joined the Georgia National Guard. My first year of college I continued to work at Taco Bell and work my reserve drill weekends until it was time for me to go to basic training. My parents paid for my tuition and I paid for my books. While at school I ended up flunking my last semester of college. I even flunked my First Aid course. I just became uninterested in school. I think I just wanted the label of being a college student.

CHAPTER 5

Military/Transitional Life

By the summer of June 1985, it was time to go to San Antonio, Texas for basic training for the Air Force . I had been on a delayed enlistment program which allowed me to work the weekend drills prior to basic training and get paid. Unfortunately, I had to go to the airport by myself. My parents did not come. I thought they should have been there, but I guess it was time for me to grow up.

I cried off and on at the airport. We did not have cellphones back then so it was not like I could call my parents while I was waiting for my flight. It was my first time away from home and I was nervous about leaving. When I finally got to San Antonio it was late at night. All I can remember is me getting off the bus with my luggage with other ladies. When I got to the dorm, I picked the bed and locker I wanted. After that I just really wanted to take a shower and go to bed. When I saw the open bay showers I was like "Ain't no way I'm going to shower in front of other women". I just decided to go to bed.

That next morning, I thought I was dreaming. It was crazy waking up to a trumpet recording playing "Reveille," but I got used to it. The training instructor came up yelling, telling us we had three minutes to get dressed and get downstairs for physical training. I quickly jumped up and put my t-shirt and shorts on and headed downstairs on the formation pad without even brushing my teeth. The ladies who were late were getting yelled at. Some even started crying which made it worse for them.

The training instructor had us pair up to do sit ups. After that was over, we got back in formation and ran as a flight around the track. We were ultimately supposed to run a mile and a half. Since basic training was six weeks long, every week they gradually increased our run by a lap. After our exercises, we would come back and shower and get ready to eat breakfast. We were eating three meals a day. I started basic training weighing 155 which was my maximum weight limit. I left basic training weighing 140. We would then go to class but everytime we were in formation, we had to carry our training book.

The first few weeks we had a lot of women set back a week because of something they did wrong. After my first week I remember in the middle of the night I saw some of the girls rushing another girl out of the shower. I later found out that she had cut her wrist in the bathroom because she could not take the training.

For me, basic training was a six-week mind game. All the yelling, you eventually got used to it. My squadron only had about nine black females. There was one female that I was attracted to and we would write letters to each other expressing how we felt toward each other. After training was over we went our separate ways.

Midway through basic training, we could go off base and have some fun. I think most of the girls and guys took that opportunity to get a room and hook up. It was a break from the hustle and bustle of training. I actually got a chance to see part of San Antonio.

Around the fourth week we had to participate in a formational parade. I was prepared and happy to be a part of the parade but at one point we had to stand at attention for a long time. One thing your training instructor told you was to not lock your knees. What did I do? I locked my knees and almost passed out. I felt myself starting to wobble but luckily we were getting ready to march back to the dorm. Now remember I was in San Antonio in the month of July which meant it was extremely hot. Around the fifth week of training, it was time to go through the obstacle course. This was an all-day thing. So, we were not able to have our regular three meals. We had to eat MREs (meals ready to eat). These were okay only because we were hungry. I did not really care for them, but it was all we had. The obstacle course was fun. It was almost two miles of running, climbing and hiking. It took the average soldier two hours to complete. I was proud to say that I got through everything without falling in the green slimy water obstacles. When basic training graduation rolled around, I chose not go because I remember going to the previous parade and almost passing out. They said that if you pass out then you would have to do an extra week so I stayed on door guard duty during the graduation. I did not want to take a chance in that Texas heat. Again, I was disappointed that my parents were not able to attend my graduation.

After basic training graduation I went to Kessler AFB in Biloxi Mississippi for six weeks of technical school. That was good because I had family there. After I got settled in, my parents came to visit along with my Aunt Missy and Uncle Edward. My parents brought me a briefcase because that is what we needed to carry our books in when we marched to class. (I still have that briefcase to this day.) In September 1985, we had Hurricane Elena come through and we had to go to a high area. We were at least 4 stories up and all I saw was water through the windows. I slept underneath a table and ate Oreo cookies. After the storm was over, we had to go and help clean up the city of Biloxi. It left a lot of busted windows and trees down. I received a Humanitarian award for helping clean up the city. Once that was done, we were able to go back to class. During this time, I met a guy who was also on base for technical school. He was from Miami Florida and his name was Bobby. We only dated while I was at Kessler AFB, but we kept in touch when I left. Graduation rolled around and it was now time to go back home to Atlanta.

Things were good for a minute when I got back home. I ended up meeting the son of one of my mom's friends and we started dating. He was a police officer for the City of East Point. Nothing too serious. I was a young 19-year-old and he was a few years older than me. While back at home things quickly changed. I remember going out for a few and coming home to my mom being upset about something. My mom had gone through my briefcase and found a letter from the female in basic training. This was definitely not a letter that two women should have written to each other. Mom and I had words about the letter and then I just left home for a few hours. I went to an active-duty recruiter and told him I wanted to go in the Air Force fulltime . I ended up going to the same recruiter who had tried to get me to go in full-time the first time but I wanted to go to school and be in the reserves. I told my mom my intentions and I spent the next two months at home before I was transferred to Langley Air Force Base in Hampton, Virginia.

November 1985, I made it to Hampton, Virginia. I had to stay in base housing for about a week because they did not have a room for me in the dorm yet. Once I got in the dorm the fun began. I worked during the day and played softball for my military unit and basketball for the base. We did a lot of traveling with the basketball team. I did not play that much but I enjoyed the traveling. I was also a member of the base Tactical Honor Guard. I was one of the pall bearers because I enjoyed the distinction of folding the flag and honoring our soldiers. I was constantly traveling but I still made a lot of friends in the dorm. Mostly guys though. I met a guy named Teddy. He kind of introduced me around the dorm. While in the dorm I did have a roommate. She was married so her husband would come up sometimes and stay in our room, but it did not bother me because I was traveling so much.

Teddy also introduced me to a girl named Kathy from Chicago who lived downstairs. She was a Senior Airman and had a room to herself. As time went on, I eventually moved in with her because she did not want just anybody moving into her room but little did she know, I had a very big crush on her. I thought I was in love with her and I was only 19. I kept those feelings inside and I remained emotionally silent.

Kathy and I got along as roommates very well. We hung out a few times but we both had our own friends. Kathy had a lot of guy friends. I was jealous of all of them whether she dated them or not. She also had friends that I would not have had anything in common with. Her friends dressed in heels and I dressed in athletic gear but sometimes we would still go to the clubs together when we could find a ride. I would not wear heels but I tried to dress like a female. A few months later I ended up buying a moped to get me around the base until my parents came to visit and brought a car for me. Once I got my car, Kathy and I could get around without having to ask for rides.

I was well liked in my unit and I can remember when my squadron commander recommended me to a Colonel to house sit on base for him and his wife and take care of their three dogs. I thought that was a very important honor. I was an airman and getting ready to housesit for a Colonel. While staying at their house on base, I can remember inviting this guy over who liked me. I just wanted him to see how important I was by showing him I was house sitting for a Colonel. While he was there his mannerisms were showing that he wanted to have sex but I was not interested. I acted like I had fallen asleep because he did not want to leave. All of a sudden I could feel him take my hand and rub on his private part. I then acted like I was waking up and he finally decided to leave. After the house sitting went well, my Colonel recommended me to house sit for a Captain off base. She even left me access to her vehicle as well. I used to drive her car sometimes just so that the guard at the gate could salute me because she had a military officer decal on her car. The most memorable moment with the captain was when I was playing in a championship softball game against her team on base. I was in right field. It was two outs; bottom of the 9th inning and my team was up by one run. There were two people on base for the captain's team. The captain was at bat. Normally, no one hits the ball to right field but I could not believe she hit the ball in the air to me. All I was saying to myself while the ball was in the air was if I catch it, she might not ask me to house sit again or if I did not catch it then my team would lose the championship. I ended up catching the ball and we won the base championship. The captain did shake my hand and congratulated me. Now that I think about it, she did not ask me to house sit for her after that.

During the rest of my stay in Virginia I was also going through a difficult transition with my sexuality. I liked men and woman. I thought something was wrong with me and at one point I wanted to be hypnotized into not being bi-sexual. I just dealt with my feelings and remained emo-tionally silent. Sometimes I would act like I was interested in guys and flirt with them even when I knew I did not like them. I was trying to hide my feelings for women but I was also trying to live up to the society norm. I did not know what kind of consequences I would have to endure if people knew I liked women. It was my believe that being a lesbian was wrong and that it was a sin and it was un-natural. I did not see it that way. I thought it was alright to like who you like. I kept that fear in my life for so long. My mental health was really being challenged. I would just mask my feelings and keep it moving. Besides, I was always busy enough to not think about my feelings.

New Year's 1987 I bought a lot of liquor to celebrate even though Kathy did not drink. I think I bought the li-quor only because I was finally old enough to buy alcohol. Kathy and I had a small party in our dorm room. I started drinking at 6:00 pm and passed out a couple of hours later. When I woke up, I felt very sick. I remember Kathy took me to the laundry room sink so that I would not throw up in our room. The laundry room was right next door to our dorm room. She said I ended up throwing up on her foot. She then got upset and sat me outside in the rain for some fresh air. I think she forgot about me because after that I remember one of the guys bringing me in and taking me to my room. Somehow, I got into my bed which was a top bunk bed. The next morning Kathy was trying to get me to eat something but I was too afraid. I did at least try to eat a burger from McDonald's.

As time went on, I started feeling more jealous about Kathy and her male friends. I had decided to move into another dorm where I had my own room. After the move, Kathy and I did not spend that much time together but we were still friends. We just started doing our own thing. I enjoyed my own room and my own car. That is until my squadron had to move into a new dorm building but I ended up with a pretty cool roommate from New Jersey named Ellie.

A month later, there was a concert in town (LL Cool J, Whodini, Beastie Boys and Run DMC). I think the venue was called the Scope. I met this very attractive guy at the concert. He was a Marine stationed at Camp LeJeune. I only remember his name as Eugene. We started dating but not for long. While dating him I felt like I was ready to have sex. He was the man I lost my virginity to. He was very gentle with me because he knew I was a virgin. It was an experience. I did not hear from him much after that but we did not part from that night in a bad way.

As time went on, I still had a tremendous crush on Kathy so I requested to be relocated because it bothered me to be around her or see her on base especially if she had a boyfriend. Kathy never knew how I felt and I was afraid to tell her. I ended up getting permanent change of station (PCS) orders to Seymour Johnson AFB, North Carolina. Before I left in April 1987, Kathy ended up going to Taegu, Korea. While in Korea, she would send me things. She sent me a Troop jacket and some Fila sneakers which were very popular then. I think I kept those shoes for the next 10 years just because she was the one that bought them for me. We tried to always stay in touch. When it was time for me to leave, my friends threw me a little get together and it was kind of sad. If I had known Kathy was leaving, I would have not put in for another base assignment but what was done was done.

April 1987, I arrived at Goldsboro, North Carolina. I continued to play softball, basketball and remain a member of the base Honor Guard. Shortly after I got to North Carolina my mother told me Demetrius had died from A.I.D.S. which was a real shock for me because I truly cared about her when I called myself dating her in high school. I had also started getting calls from the East Point police officer who was about to get married but he just wanted me to come home so we could sleep together before he said, "I do". That was never going to happen.

At work I had become good friends with a co-worker

named Rachelle from California. She was married and had a son. She made me her sons' godmother. His name was Marcus and he was 3 years old. While I was stationed at Seymour Johnson, I got in contact with my friend Bobby from Keesler. We started dating off and on again. I was stationed with his sister and he was stationed in South Carolina. But then there was another guy named Tommy who I actually started dating as well and broke up with Bobby. Rachelle introduced us. We were intimate a couple of times. At one point I thought I was pregnant because I got very sick one morning at work and was throwing up. I was not using any condoms with any of the guys that I had slept with. I only trusted my birth control pills to work. I was not even thinking about catching any STDs. I guess I was exceptionally lucky. The pregnancy was a false alarm. Tommy and I dated a couple of months then Bobby worked his way back into the picture and I stopped seeing Tommy. Then Bobby and I broke up and I started dating Tommy again. Hell, I did not know what I wanted at the time. I just knew it was normal to have a boyfriend. I think I was also making myself try and like sex with a man.

Summertime came and it was time for softball. My team played on base but we also travelled. I really liked my coach, Pop Jenkins. His wife, Gladys, was our hind catcher. He had four children. We had become such good friends that he started inviting me and another player named Tracey to his house. We were sort of adopted by their family. We are still close 34 years later. A few months later, I had volunteered to go to Osan Korea for a few months for Team Spirit 1988. I took my car to Atlanta while I was overseas. I had also contacted Kathy who was already in Korea and told her when I would arrive. The plane ride was very long. I did not care much for the flying but I got through it. We first flew from North Carolina to St Louis then to California. From there we flew to Hawaii and stayed over a couple of hours. Then we flew to a place called Wake Island to refuel. Our last stop was Korea. We were on a cargo plane (C141) that had parachute seats. There is a row up against the walls of the plane then you are sitting across (knee to knee) from someone on parachute seats. Then their backs were against someone who was knee to knee with someone across from them. Not much walking room in the aisles and we also had cargo in the rear. There were no windows. In order to get our bag lunch, they had to pass it down the aisle.

When we arrived at Osan, I stepped off the plane and it was very cold. We were set to live in tent city but it was not ready so we had to stay in a hotel and pay for it also. I had to get my Sergeant to contact my parents because I did not realize I would have to pay to stay. My folks wired me some money. After a couple of days, we were ready to move into our tents. I had already found some of my friends I used to be stationed with and hung out with them a lot when I was not at work.

Now back to tent city. I was the lowest ranking person in my tent, so I was the go-fer. I got so tired of going to get kerosene for our heater, bathing in a portable shower, and using port-a-potty. I ended up staying in the dorm with one of my friends. She had an extra bed so that was cool.

Korea was so fascinating. The clubs were interesting also. The restroom in the clubs were co-ed and literally a hole in the floor. You would squat over a hole. The alcohol was very strong . The music was six months behind but we still enjoyed it. We actually partied at a club called, "Soul Train". The shopping was also the great. I was not into dressy clothes so I had alot of sweat suits made and I bought a lot of sneakers. One thing about me, I love athletic gear and my sneakers had to match my sweatsuit.

Now it was time to catch up with Kathy so I went to visit her. I was stationed at Osan and she was stationed at Taegu. That was a couple of hours away from me. The train ride was something else. The cashiers did not speak English but they understood money. All you had to do was tell the cashier where you wanted to go and they gave you a ticket.

Kathy had her own apartment so I at least had somewhere to stay. At the time Kathy had a boyfriend. Again, I still had a crush on her and I was jealous of any person in her life like that. I wanted to tell her how I felt but with the boyfriend in the way I kind of felt like she was not going to accept my feelings and maybe even be upset and not be friends with me anymore. I kept "emotionally silent" and just enjoyed my time with my friend until it was time for me to go back to Osan.

During my stay at Osan, Kathy came to visit me. I was excited that she was coming. I had gotten a hotel room for her so that she would have a place to stay overnight. The day had come and I was very anxious. I looked all over for Kathy that day and night. It was not like we had cellphones back then so I had no way of contacting her. Something told me to check other hotels and see if she had gotten her own room because she had no way of knowing that I had a room for her. Some kind of way I found her at another hotel. I went to her room just to catch up with her and I noticed her boyfriend was with her. I did not know he was coming. I thought I was going to spend some time with just my friend. I told her that I had gotten her a room. She apologized and I said that it was okay and then I left. Needless to say, I was very upset inside. I ended up giving the room to one of my co-workers. I was so sad. Again, I remained "emotionally silent".

So, the next day I met up with Kathy and I accompanied her and her boyfriend to the train station so that they could go back. I sat in the back seat with Kathy. Her boyfriend was in the front seat with the driver. When we got to the train station I did not want her to leave. I only saw her one more time before it was time for me to go back to the United States. Again, I thought I was in still in love with her but maybe it was just infatuation. I just felt I loved Kathy beyond words.

Now it was time for me to go back to the states just in time to find out Tommy had fallen for a girl who worked at Popeye's chicken. I guess it was expected because I did him so wrong. I was also back in the states with no car. Ever since the 9th grade I always wanted a BMW. I told my parents and they said that they would look for one for me in Atlanta but I told them I wanted to buy it. A couple of months went by and my parents called and said that they think they found the kind of BMW I wanted. I flew to Atlanta to stay at least a week to give me enough time to buy the car myself. When I arrived in Atlanta, my parents came to pick me up from the airport. When I got to the parking lot my dad asked me if I wanted to drive and I said sure. I started looking for their Chevy Blazer that they had at the time but did not see it. I finally asked them, "Where is the truck?" Next thing I know they pointed at a brown BMW and gave me the key. I went crazy in the parking lot. I started crying and everything. They had bought the car for me but naturally I had to pay the car note and they took care of the insurance. I did not make enough money to pay for both. I was so damn happy. As soon as I got back to North Carolina, I started my car note allotment straight to my parents' account. I think my note was $275 a month. As an Airman First Class, I only made $875 a month. When I got back to the base, everyone was trying to figure out how an Airman First Class could afford a 1984 (318i) BMW in 1988. My car was never dirty. I washed it every week. Guys were really trying to date me after that but I was really not interested. I picked back up playing my sports, going to work and going to the club on the weekends. Tracey and I continued to play on the same softball and basketball team. By this time, I believe Pop Jenkins and his family had changed duty stations.

CHAPTER 6

Rape

The day I was raped by a friend. I met him at the Non-Commissioned Officers (NCO) club shortly after my return from Osan, Korea in 1988. He seemed like a cool guy. We became friends with no interest of dating. It felt like we were childhood friends who would just hang out sometimes. It was a normal day for me and my friend, a person I thought was like a brother to me. It was not unusual for us to just go hang out at the mall or movies or even in each other's room. However, this one day would change my life forever. I never saw it coming.

We had spent the day together and that evening we had gone to the movies. Afterwards, we went to my room just to hang out. We were sitting on the bed in my room watching TV then suddenly, he started rubbing on my leg. I thought he was just kidding around. Then he started moving his hand up my inner thigh and I just played it off and told him to stop playing. When he would not stop, I got up and walked toward the door and asked him to leave. When he got up, instead of leaving, all of a sudden, he pushed me up against the locker with his forearm across my chest and the knob on the locker pressing against the middle of my back. Again, I asked him to stop. He just kept forcibly putting his hand between my legs. I tried to push him off of me but I was not strong enough and too scared to scream. He told me if I stop fighting him he would not hurt me any further. I stopped trying to fight. He made me undress from the waist down and get on my bed. He then got on top of me, forced my legs open and thrust his penis inside of me. It was extremely painful. I instantly felt the pressure. He kept telling me to relax. He wanted me to react to him but I just laid there waiting for him to finish. I did not have a roommate at the time so I guess he felt comfortable enough to take his time and not worry about anyone walking in the room. After what felt like eternity, I guess he could not have an orgasm because I was not responding to him sexually. I just kept asking him to stop, but all he kept telling me was to just relax and loosen up. I kept telling him he was hurting me but he ignored me. The more I asked him to stop, the faster and harder he would penetrate me.

By this time, I was very numb. He finally got up

and left like he had done nothing wrong. Once he left my room, I got up and went immediately to the bathroom. I tried to urinate but it burnt so bad. He had literally penetrated me until my vagina was raw. I tried to put some vaseline around my labia so that it would not burn so bad. When I would wipe, I could also see blood on the tissue from the torn walls of my vagina. Afterwards I quickly got in the shower. The burning sensation was so painful and all I wanted to do was wash him off of me. All I could do after showering was lay on the floor. I think I slept on my floor for the next few days. I would go to work every day as if my life was fine. I hated to urinate because my vagina stayed raw for about a week after this incident.

I never saw him again because he was gone a lot with his job. I never told anyone until 23 years later. I did not think anyone would believe me if I had said something. My career intentions were to stay in the Air Force and ultimately become a member of the United States Honor Guard in Washington, DC. I had completed my package to apply for the Honor Guard but after this incident I did not think it was worth it. After my enlistment was up, I chose to get out of the military because staying in the military would have not been in my best interest. I felt that I would have been labeled.

I later found myself avoiding men except at work be-

cause I had no choice but to be around them. I was still attracted to men because that is what society recognizes as a normal
relationship. I did not even tell my friend Tracey. Tracey and I
later became roommates after this incident. Tracey and I had
become very close through playing sports and later we started
having an attraction toward one another. I think maybe she
had lesbian tendencies even though she was engaged to a man.

Tracey was a few years older than me and she became
the first woman I was intimate with. It only happened a few
times because I felt our friendship was more important.

I felt like I could not see myself ever having sex with
a man again. Tommy and Bobby were before the rape and
they were the only men who were gentle with me during
sex. I call it sex because I had never experienced love making
with a man.

October 1989 was when it was time for me to start getting ready to get out of the military. It was in the middle of
basketball season and the team celebrated me by giving me a
cake with individual square slices with every player's name on
it and mini-Coors Lite beer cans on each one. I used to drink
Coors Lite after the games. It was a sad goodbye. Meanwhile
Tracey and I had discussed her coming to Atlanta to work
and we could be roommates. She was scheduled to get out in
January 1990.

CHAPTER 7

Life After Military

When I got back to Atlanta, I had decided to go to Macon to look for a job. I went for about a week and stayed in a hotel. I was also finishing up my two-year reserve obligation at Warner Robins Air Force Base. That is why I chose Macon to try to reside in. Unfortunately, I could not find anything. The military did not set me up for civilian world after my honorable discharge. They did not provide any resources to help me acclimate back to civilian life. There was no guidance or assistance offered to veterans to help them find employment once they separated. I ended up not working and drawing unemployment for the next three months. However, prior to me separating from the military, I was at least able to purchase furniture for my future apartment. The military was storing it for six months. I was determined not to have to live with my parents; I also thought I would have enough money to survive when I got out but I had heavy credit card debt, at least 10 credit cards. So, I had no choice but to move back home while I search for employment.

January 1990 rolled around and I was waiting to hear about a job opening from my mother's friend who worked for the city of East Point. Her friend was the East Point police officers' mother. After I came back home, the police officer tried to get back with me and I guess finish what he started. By now he was separated from his wife. Again, I told him "No".

Now toward the end of January, Tracey got out of the military and my mom agreed to let her live with us but did not know we had an intimate relationship. I really appreciated my parents for allowing her to stay but I was still ready to get my own place. In February, our military basketball coach called us to see if we wanted to play in a basketball tournament at Shaw Air Force Base in South Carolina so we went. We were leaving very early on a Saturday morning so I took some No-Doze to stay awake. I believe we got eliminated from the basketball tournament but I enjoyed playing again. When we got back, I could not go to sleep because the No-Doze kept me up from Saturday to Monday. No matter how hard I tried to close my eyes, I just could not go to sleep. I vowed never to take it again. About a week later, I had an interview for the job I was waiting on as a Crime Scene Technician with the City of East Point. I had only one interview skirt suit because that is how I was supposed to dress for a job interview according to society. If I could have worn a sweat suit I would have. The following week, the job offer had finally come through. I was so happy. I think it only paid $7.20/hour but I did not care. Between my last unemployment check and my first paycheck, I was able to get an apartment because I wanted my own space. My parents were not charging us to live there and I appreciated them very much.

Once I started working, I found that I really enjoyed working crime scenes. My primary job was to fingerprint suspects, take crime scene photos and dust for fingerprints at crime scenes. My first crime scene call was to go to the morgue to fingerprint a suspect who was shot and killed by an Atlanta Police officer. I was nervous but excited. I watch a lot of gory movies so I looked at things like a movie. I can remember the medical technician bringing the body out. It had a plastic bag over the head and the bag was full of blood. When I looked at his hands, you could see rigor mortis had set in and his fingers were curved under. In order to fingerprint him for identity purposes, I had to literally break his fingers to get his fingerprints. Once they compared the prints in a data base it was found that the suspect was one of America's Ten Most Wanted out of Philadelphia.

On one of my burglary cases, the fingerprints I obtained led to the conviction of a suspect. I received a commendation from the detective of that case. Another week I responded to a call of a person shot. When I got to the scene, I noticed a body in the middle of the street. The body was not covered and there were people from the neighborhood standing around. It was my job to go and take crime scene photos so that I could cover the body up until the coroner arrived. The crowd was getting very agitated because the police just had the male body lying in the street. That was my first murder scene and I will never forget the young man or his name. Another crime scene that I will never forget was a welfare check on a female. It was the middle of July and the temperatures were extremely hot that week. When I got to the home, I noticed the officers had the windows open. Once I went inside the home, I found out why they were open. A female had died in her home and was possibly in the home for at least 3 days with no air condition flowing through the home. It was later determined that the woman had a heart attack and had collapsed behind her bathroom door face down. After I took the initial crime scene photos, I had to turn the body over and take more photos. Once I turned her body over, there was a smell I will never forget. One of the officers vomited from the smell. I just held my breathe in between taking photos. The smell would not come out of your clothes once contact was made.

By this time, Tracey had found a temporary job. Her job looked promising and could turn into a permanent one. We had moved into a two-bedroom, two-bathroom apartment for $500 a month in Union City. It was quite nice. Shortly after we moved in, I got a Cocker Spaniel and my mom named him Dusty. He was so bad but so sweet. Meanwhile I had to drive to Robins Air Force Base in Macon one weekend out of the month for my reserve obligation. I also had a yearly two-week obligation as well and I had a choice of where I wanted to go. My first year I chose Keesler AFB because my aunt Missy lived near there. She was one of my favorite aunts.

I worked one week of my reserve duty there and then I drove to San Antonio Texas to visit Kathy for a week. My mother did not know I was going to San Antonio. I was afraid to tell her so I lied and said I was going to be at Keesler Air Force Base for both weeks. I was still afraid to have conversations with my mom even as an adult. I continued to remain emotionally silent.

After my week with my family, I left early in the morning so I could be able to pick Kathy up at the San Antonio Airport. She was flying back from Chicago and I knew it would take me at least 12 hours to drive there from Mississippi. I was so excited to see her. I still had that same crush on her that I had from day one when I met her.

After that drive, I was really tired. I thought this was going to be the visit where I finally tell her how I feel about her. I think she kind of knew how I felt but did not want to have a discussion about it. I did not say anything so I made the best of the visit. I was just glad to be around Kathy. My first night there we started reminiscing about the time I got drunk and threw up on her foot in the dorm at Langley. While at Kathy's I called home to check on Tracey and she told me Dusty had jumped from the car while she was driving. He had broken his leg. She also told me she told my mother I was in Texas so now I would have to hear my mom fussing when I got back home to Georgia. My week quickly came and went and it was time for me to go back to Atlanta. Again, I did not want to leave Kathy but I had to. That was a very long trip back but I am glad I made it home safely.

CHAPTER 8

First Job/First Relationship

When I got back to work, I met a female officer named Diane. I knew she was a lesbian. At the time I did not know about certain terminologies in the gay lifestyle. I can remember her asking me if I was family, meaning (lesbian). I asked her what did that mean, so she left it alone thinking I was not a lesbian. Even though I dabbled in the lifestyle before, I did not know much about being a lesbian. I just thought it was about two people of the same gender dating each other because marriage was not legal between same sex couples at this time. At first I was concentrating on the physical aspect of that type of relationship because I was looking for love. I just thought the pain I felt from my military sexual assault was something I could not feel by being with a woman. I soon learned that at least the mental aspect of this type of relationship was no different than a heterosexual relationship.

There was also another female officer named Alexis who kind of took me under her wings at work since I was a new female at the police department. She would tell me who to trust and who to watch out for. While at work I remember an incident where I went to fingerprint an inmate and a white female officer brought a Black male offender in the booking area. He was very drunk and just running his mouth being belligerent. He got verbally aggressive with the female officer and started disrespecting her with his words. The desk sergeant (white male officer) at the time grabbed a handle (like the handle from a wooden hammer) and hit the Black male in the head. The next day he had a huge bump on his head. I just know that did not come from one strike. I pulled up the report and it was doctored up like I assumed it would be. I never realized things like that was still happening.

After a few months on the job, some of the other male officers started talking about me in a way that they wanted to know who would be the first to have sex with me. That is when Alexis came to me and had a talk with me. She was kind of a prissy officer but I knew she could handle her business when it came down to it. After a while I started getting the hang of the job. My supervisor was really cool. It was my Lieutenant I did not care for. He played favorites. After about a year, I attempted to take the police officers' exam but I was told I did not pass. I think my Lieutenant did not want me to grow within the department. I was bitter about it but at least I already had a job.

Now back to Diane. I started trying to befriend her since I knew she was a lesbian but she took it as me trying to date her which was far from the truth. What I did not know was that Alexis and Diane were dating during this time. I would have never thought Alexis was her girlfriend so I let it be known that I only wanted to be friends with the both of them. Now since Alexis was a Black female and older, I looked to her as a person who could give me some insight on the lesbian lifestyle as a black female. The more Alexis and I talked the more Diane thought I was trying to hook up with Alexis. I did not know their relationship was kind of rocky during this time. As time went on and as Diane and Alexis's relationship was getting worse, both me and Alexis started getting closer and eventually started having feelings for one another that was more than just friendship. Because of this I would have disagreements with Diane every now and then. The more they fought the more I was trying to make Alexis my girlfriend. I found out Alexis had two sons. Me and her youngest son became really close. The oldest one I don't think cared for me much but we got along the best we could for as long as we could.

One day I was on my way to work when I noticed an overturned car on the highway. I pulled over to make sure everyone was alright. I noticed a lady in the vehicle. She did not appear to have any visible injuries. I told her not to move. I used my police radio to let my dispatch know about the accident and to send jurisdictional police and an ambulance. Once they arrived on scene, I left. I often wondered what happened to the lady. I just hoped she was not seriously hurt. I believe coming up on the accident made me really want to be a police officer so I never gave up trying.

While living with Tracey she received military orders to be deployed to Dessert Storm. Without her help I could not afford the apartment by myself so I had to move to a one bedroom in Riverdale, Georgia. It was a nice cozy apartment. It was $385 a month and it was closer to my job. It was then when Alexis and I really started dating officially and she had stopped seeing Diane. She came over for a first official date and I took her to Kentucky Fried Chicken. This was also our first kiss. Throughout the beginning of the relationship, I had to go through some turmoil with Diane but it eventually stopped. After that I would pretty much spend more time at Alexis's house. My parents did not know about Alexis. For the most part, I pretty much kept my life private from my parents because I did not think they would understand. I also thought they would not have anything else to do with me. I actually thought they would disown me so I remained emotionally silent.

When I did finally think it was time to stop hiding, I decided to tell my parents but it was not face to face. One day I saw an article in an issue of "Essence" about a mother and daughter. The editor was telling her story of being a lesbian and her mother was telling how she dealt with it. I sent the article to my mother. She read the article but afterwards I don't remember her speaking to me for a while. My dad was always there even though he may not have approved. I was always going to be daddy's little girl no matter what.

After living in my apartment for about 6 months, I moved in with Alexis because I was not making enough money to pay all those credit card bills from when I separated from the military. Meanwhile I had started having contact with Kathy again. I told Kathy I was dating Alexis and I think that bothered her. I told her that I was happy. After that conversation, I lost contact with Kathy around 1991.

Now I thought the Diane drama was done but she was still hanging around. I can remember an incident when I tried to call Alexis but she would not answer the phone. I left work because I was worried. When I got home, I found

Diane on my porch talking to Alexis. When I walked up to the door, she decided to leave.

Another episode involved Alexis and her family. They were also a handful. One night while I was at work, her mother and her two brothers went over to our home to discourage our relationship. Her youngest brother tried to convince Alexis that he and I were intimate in our bed and her mother was talking about how wrong the relationship was. Her oldest brother was a little more subtle. Alexis said she had to put her family out of our house. Eventually everyone accepted us to the point where I was invited to family functions.

Now Alexis's youngest son was scared of Dusty so eventually I had to give Dusty away. I ended up giving him to a friend of Alexis who had kids. That was a sad day for me because I was used to having a dog since a young age. After a couple of months, Alexis saw that I missed my dog. We went to a pet store in the mall just to look at dogs. I picked up the most precious white Poodle but she cost $500 so I put her back. The next day Alexis said let's go get the dog. At the time, I did not know she pawned one of her rings to get me the dog. I found out about the pawn one day while she was not home and they called and said she was past due on her payment. That was one of the best things anyone had ever done for me. We named the Poodle "Precious" and she was 8 weeks old.

After about two years of being together we bought a home. It was a tri-level three-bedroom two and half bath home with an in-ground pool. It was a beautiful home. At the time we paid $74,500 for it. We also adopted another Poodle. This one was a male and he was five years old. His name was Champ. He fit right into the family. Precious had to get use to him because she was spoiled. I loved my dogs very much. I thought we were all one big happy family. Everything in the home was going well until the oldest son starting disrespecting Alexis. I told her I could not sit back and watch him disrespect her. I told her it was time for him to live with his dad. She agreed it was time especially since he was almost a teenager . By this time, we were no longer working with the Police Department. We both started working at Michelin College. It was here where I started working as a security officer. This was also a way for me to get into the police academy to become a police officer. I think everyone at work knew we were a couple but they did not say anything. We always conducted ourselves professionally. Police officers did not get too much respect working at the collegiate level even though we went through the same training as any other police officer in the state of Georgia. When I went through the academy, the course was only 6 weeks long. I was very interested in the being a cop so I took it very seriously. After I graduated, I later became the day watch supervisor. It was during this time that I met a Lieutenant from our neighboring Hillman College. I was on campus one day when Alexis called me in the office. Hillman Lt. Smith was inquiring on a case dealing with students from Michelin College but some way a conversation about our lifestyle came up prior to me getting to the office. One conversation led to another and we became friends with Lt. Smith and her girlfriend.

I spent about a year and a half working for Michelin College then an opportunity to work at Hillman College for more money came up and I took it. Now I was working with Lt Smith. She was actually my supervisor. As I got to know her, she struck me as a person I considered to be a cheater. She would keep a toothbrush in our work file cabinet and it was not for brushing her teeth after a meal.

I actually got caught with being involved with a student. I can remember one night during my shift I was intimate with one of the basketball players. I knew I was wrong but I did not care at the time. If I could get away with it then I would do it. When I got home that night, for some reason Alexis wanted a kiss as soon as I arrived. She smelled the woman perfume on me and questioned me about it. I went berserk and tried to make it seem like I had not done anything wrong and that I had not been with another woman. I even tried to show anger and punched a picture frame and ended up cutting my hand. I guess I was hoping that by doing that it would stop the conversation at hand.

I was never good at conversing during an argument. It had gotten so bad to the point that I moved out of the house for about a month. I think I was trying to play the field. I remember one evening I went to get the basketball player and bring her over to my new place. Alexis also showed up. Can you say awkward? We were not doing anything. Alexis just stood there in the living room. I finally told Alexis I was going to take her back to Hillman and we could talk about everything in the morning. She agreed. This was also around the time where I did not like how my life was going and just could not take it. This was when I tried to commit suicide. I think that was my way of getting sympathy and making things go away. I decided to take a bunch of pills. I did it while I was at work. I was driving around in the patrol car and I pulled over and took the pills. The pills just made me very sleepy. I called Alexis and told her I was tired. Eventually I was able to recoup from that ordeal. Meanwhile Alexis and I got back together for a short period.

After the basketball player graduated, I had no further communication with her. I was still working with Lt. Smith but I later found out that she was telling my every move to Alexis because she was no longer with her girlfriend and she really wanted a relationship with Alexis. The final straw was when Alexis told me Lt. Smith had made a pass at her. She also showed me a letter that Lt. Smith had written to her telling her all the things they could have together. She showed me the letter while I was at work. I went berserk on Lt. Smith. I was working the front entry gate of the campus and did not care who heard me talking loudly. I showed Lt.Smith the letter she gave Alexis. She snatched it, laughed and went and put it in the trunk of her car. When she walked away, I had to regroup because I had to remember I was at work. The next day I quit. I had briefly gotten a part-time job at Toys R Us because it was around Christmas time. I had also worked for Delta Airlines loading luggage onto the planes. I resigned from Delta because it was too strenuous but I was still working at the toy store because it was the only job I had at the time.

Coach/Deputy Sheriff

Since I had time on my hands I decided to coach youth sports at a local recreation center. The first sport I coached was tee-ball. Now that was a funny sight; trying to coach 4 and 5-year-olds whose attention spans were extremely short. Most of my players could not even pronounce the word "coach" so they called me "toach.". I think we won one game out of ten but to the kids we won all our games. I still have the winning baseball from our only victory in 1993. The team was co-ed. I had one special needs child on the team. He was about 6 or 7. He pretty much needed one on one attention with coaching. He also had a crush on me. It was kind of hard coaching him when all he wanted to do was chase me all over the field. He almost went through the whole season without getting a hit. During one of the later games in the season he finally got that hit and everyone stood up and cheered. He got a home run out of it but it was the way he got it. After he hit the ball he just stood at the plate. When I told him to run, he ran to 3rd base, then 2nd base, then 1st base and then home plate. It was still a homerun to me. I think we lost that game by 22 points but I told the team we won. One of my girls on the team could really play and the other one had potential. I had her playing in the outfield but I had to keep picking her up out of the grass all the time in the field. I would put her in her position in the outfield and then by the time I got back to the dugout she would be sitting in the grass playing. Then when the ball would come to her, she would get up, run to get the ball and then just chase the batter around the bases. It was hilarious and fun.

After that season was over, I started playing softball for a women's team with the same recreational center. After softball I started coaching 8 and 9-year-old co-ed basketball. I was very nervous about coaching basketball for the first time even though it was really what I wanted to coach. My first year I had a young man on my team whose mother was in the military and he also had an older brother who played for the Pittsburgh Steelers. At first his mother had so much negativity toward my coaching technique. My thing was that you teach them the fundamentals first. I pretty much did not listen to her and coached the way I wanted to coach.

One of my players fathers volunteered to help me coach and Alexis was team mom. I was the only female coach in that age group. That year we had an 8-2 record. We also had a rival team we always played against; their coach was a friend of mine who worked for the recreation center. He had the Lakers and we were the Warriors. We played each team twice. We lost both games to the Lakers. It was a good rivalry that lasted for the next 4 years. One season my mom helped me coach. We both played basketball in high school and we both enjoyed the kids. I may not have done a lot with my mom when I was young but I enjoyed coaching with her as an adult. She was the disciplinarian and score keeper. That year we had a 7 - 3 record. One thing I would do with all my players was teach them the importance of keeping their grades up in school.

My last year coaching, my team finished 9-1. We had finally beaten the Lakers at least once that year. I also coached a girls' team during the summer. I was proud of my coaching style. I was a coach who never sat down during a game. You would have thought I was coaching an NBA team. The next few years I continued to play softball for the recreation center. It was while I was playing softball that I met a girl named Tammy. We became friends through softball. In 1995, I was hired by Clayton County Sheriff Department and then my work schedule would not allow me to continue coaching.

Clayton County Sheriff Department was my first real police job and the place where I met my soon-to-be best friend/sister Alison. She worked in the bonding office. I worked 12-hour shifts in the jail which was good. If I wanted to take a week off, then I would only have to take 2 days off during that week. I would be scheduled off on Monday and Tuesday then work Wednesday and Thursday, then I would be off again on Friday, Saturday and Sunday, therefore only having to take off on Wednesday and Thursday for a full week off.

I enjoyed working in the jail. I got the hang of it very quickly. The only thing I did not like about it was when I would have to dress the female inmates out in their jail uniforms. Believe it or not, I did not like looking at those naked women. Plus, I had to strip them down and then spray their private parts with a type of bug spray to keep crabs out of the cells from unclean women. I really thought that was degrading but I understood why it had to be done. After a few months of working there, I just had the ladies spray themselves if they wanted to.

When I first started training I was kind of scared. I had to actually go into the sections (men and women) and conduct a head count. I was getting whistled at from day one from the men and women. It was embarrassing. I had several female inmates trying to pass me letters because they liked me. When I would work in the tower/pod they would all want to come up to the window for something just to try to leave me a note. I had even been investigated by Internal Affairs about me fraternizing with an inmate. I was a nice deputy and I felt like if you did not mess over me then I had no reason to be unfair to you. I did have certain inmates who would look out for me and listen out for things concerning other deputies. One of the inmates was a girl named Renee. She was the main one who would let me know when there was going to be a problem in the women's cells. In other words, she was a snitch.

I can remember an incident with an inmate named Louise. She kept putting in a request to retrieve a certain type of lotion that she needed that was in her property bin. This day I just happened to be working as the property deputy when I got the request. Louise was a regular inmate and I did not have any problems with her. But for some reason or another she really needed this lotion. I went to her property bin and got the lotion. Something told me to look inside the bottle before I gave it to her. I poured the lotion out into another container and I found something wrapped in a dark plastic bag. When I opened the plastic bag there was another clear plastic bag that contained a marijuana cigarette. I then looked on her paperwork to see who left the lotion for her and it was her sister. I then had a warrant issued for her sister's arrest because it was illegal to bring drugs into the jail. Now I was on Louise's bad list because her sister was picked up on the warrant.

After this incident, I remember having a run-in with Louise regarding her inmate girlfriend. Her girlfriend told another inmate that she had an interest in me and Louise did not like that at all. Inmates liking Deputies was not unusal in the jail. One of the inmates told me Louise was talking about jumping me when I came to do the next headcount. It had been a while since I was assigned to do headcount in the women's pod. One night before headcount I just happened to listen in on the conversation in the pod through the overhead speaker. I heard Louise talking about how she was going to jump me when I came in her section. So, after listening to her over the intercom I told her that I will see her for headcount.

So, when it came time for me to do headcount, I did their section last on purpose. Louise was in a downstairs room which had a cell door that did not lock. The environment was not really safe, which is why I chose to treat the inmates like human beings so that I would not get injured by being mean to any of them. When I started my headcount in Louise section, I chose to do the floor headcount first because we were overcrowded. There were inmates laying on the floor on mats. I then went upstairs and then came down-stairs; the level that Louise was on. She was about the fourth room over from my starting point. I checked the rooms by looking into the cell doors and making sure the inmate was there and alert. By this time everyone was waiting on me to get to Louise's room.

I finally stepped in front of her room not knowing what was going to happen. I looked inside the room and she did not say a word to me. I then slowly finished doing headcount giving her an opportunity to jump me. I think she knew the other ladies were not going to allow her to do that. That was the last of Louise; for now.

By this time Alexis had befriended an old school bud-dy named Evelyn, so I thought. Evelyn was in a relationship with a female. We started hanging out a lot. Evelyn's rela-tionship was not good with her girlfriend but they pretended it was. During this time Louise had gotten out of jail. One evening myself, Alexis, Evelyn and her girlfriend went to get something to eat at a local Steak and Shake. Guess who was working in the back making the milkshakes. It was Louise. That girl really caused a scene in the restaurant.

She saw me and came up front to where we were, which was at the bar in front of the restaurant, talking cra-zy and I just looked at her and laughed. I guess she was still upset with me because I had her sister arrested. Her co-workers were trying to get her to go back in the back but she refused to as long as I was sitting at the counter. She even threw some ketchup packages at one of her co-workers because she was upset. We got our food and left but not before I told the manager about her arrested.

After we got home, Alexis called back up to the restaurant and ultimately Louise was fired. A couple of months later, guess who comes back to jail. Yes, Louise. I was the one to dress her out. I thought that was funny and I smiled the whole time.

I have never had any other run-ins with inmates except with one who was refusing to go back to her cell from the infirmary. I had asked her several times but she refused. When she kept refusing, I went to grab her arm to escort her to her cell. She then threw water in my face and all I could do was swing and catch her in the throat. Another deputy then came down and we cuffed her and placed her in solitaire.

I had a good friend at the Sheriff Department who was the first straight woman that I told I was gay. Her name was Tyra. She was a secretary for our team. We kind of looked out for each other. For the most part, the deputies that I worked with were nice. There was one deputy who was kind of a male chauvinist. He was very stereotypical especially when it came to lesbians. He was a Sergeant within the department. Believe it or not no one really knew whether I was gay or straight. I even drove a male friend's truck to work sometimes so that people would think I was driving a boyfriend's vehicle. Again, covering up my true self and being emotionally silent.

The Sergeant was the only one who would have something to say about lesbian stereotypes. He was dumb enough to use certain terms around me and Tyra. He would even talk to Tyra about me. Like I said before, Tyra and I looked after each other and she told me what the Sergeant was saying. I then went to personnel to file a complaint based on things he said to me and the things he said to Tyra. Personnel did see that I had enough to file a departmental harassment complaint and a hearing was set. When we went to the hearing he came with an attorney. Tyra gave a statement on my behalf. It was determined he was out of line with the way he was talking to me. It was defined as sexual harassment. I did not know how far I could have pursued it. He only got suspended for a couple of days without pay. I did see him several times after that when he would bring a prisoner into intake but no words were said.

During this time, I had an extra job working at a skating rink in Jonesboro, Georgia. I worked on a night where there was a bunch of teenagers. Some of them were very unruly. I found that out when a teenager told me another teen had a gun. When I went to approach the teen he ran out one of the exit doors. I gave chase and ended up in an apartment complex. I did not know my exact location so I went back to the skating rink before I had gotten hurt or shot. I was also a part of the Clayton County Sheriff Honor Guard. We attended several law enforcements details. I loved being on the Honor Guard ever since the military. My Sergeant was cool. He was prior military and very professional about the Honor Guard. He also took me under his wing professionally.

I remember accidently releasing an inmate by mistake. After we found out about it, I told the Sergeant and he said put your gun belt on. Myself, Sergeant and two other deputies went to the inmate's home address, two of us in the front and two of us in the back. Fortunately, the inmate was there and he also knew he was not supposed to be released. I got out of that one thanks to Sergeant.

Now by this time Alexis and I started growing apart again. I can remember an incident where I had to work at the skating rink. I left for work but forgot my flashlight. Alexis mentioned she had to work at the Atlanta Motor Speedway because by this time she worked for Atlanta Police Department. When I went back to get my flashlight I think I kind of startled her. She had peeped her head outside the bathroom door where she was getting ready for work but I noticed she was putting on some make-up. She did not normally put on make-up when she went to work. I also noticed she had on dressy clothes. I did not think anything else of it so I just grabbed my flashlight and went to work. I did not know at that time she was meeting up with someone and not actually going to work. We had really grown apart so I decided to move. I moved in with my dad for a few months. By this time, my parents had divorced.

I was still friends with Evelyn and I would talk to her about what was going on with me and Alexis. What I did not know was that her and her girlfriend had broken up. The more we talked the more Evelyn would start telling me things about Alexis. She told me she was not an old school buddy of hers. She met her on a dating site. I did not know that Alexis was searching on a dating site. Evelyn also told me she was not the first-person Alexis had met on the site. The more Evelyn was telling me, the more upset I was getting. She also told me I should get an A.I.D.S. test because of Alexis. I just could not believe what I was hearing. I cheated first with the Hillman basketball player and then Alexis had started cheating with women on a dating site. Evelyn also convinced me to sign over the house to her since it was in both of our names and the fact that I was no longer living there. Maybe Evelyn was working with Alexis to get me to do that. I don't know.

I did not know what to do or what to believe. I did everything Evelyn suggested I do. But when Alexis sold the house, I did not get anything from the sale because I literally gave up my rights to the home. I was so dumb and naïve. Shortly after that, Evelyn and I starting getting closer to the point where we started dating. By this time, I was working with McDonough Police Department and I was working nights. The relationship was fun in the beginning. I spent a lot of time with her. She used to write me little notes telling me that she loved me. I think I kept every one. I know it may not have been the best timing to get involved again so quickly but I was angry and I wanted to get back at Alexis. With me now staying with my dad, I only had to pay one bill. This meant I had money because I got paid every week. Evelyn always wanted to go out and eat or go somewhere because I would always pay for it. The problem came when I told Evelyn I was getting ready to move into my own place. She knew I would have less money because now I would have rent and my own bills to pay. After that, all of a sudden she wanted to see other people. It came out the blue. Unbeknownst to me she was still doing dating sites and had met someone named Piper. I did not know this until one day I drove by her house after I got off work and a strange car would be in the driveway at 6 o'clock in the morning. I was so hurt.

I tried talking to her but she said she just wanted to be friends. I guess my money ran out. But it did not run out until after I bought her a $500 ring from the pawn shop. I did not have a problem with her having it and she did take it. I had accepted the fact that she did not want to be with me. I accepted the fact that she wanted to be friends and we communicated as friends.

While she was dating Piper, she would tell me about Piper's ex-girlfriend Aubree. She said the girl was trouble and that she steals people's identities and apply for credit cards. She was saying she was bad news. Meanwhile, Evelyn had gotten fired from her job so she started calling me more. On one of those calls she asked me if I could pay her phone bill. I was still a friend even though she did me wrong so I put $100 in a hallmark card. She said thank you and that was that.

When it was time for me to move into my own place, I moved into a one-bedroom in Morrow, Georgia. I was still working for McDonough Police Department but I also had a part-time job at Kirkland's in the mall. Since I was single and not seeing anyone, all I did was work. A few months later it was close to the holidays. I spent thanksgiving with my parents. It was going good for me for a minute while I was alone. Meanwhile Alexis started dating

my friend Tammy. Tammy had moved in the house Alexis
and I once shared. That was surprising.

CHAPTER 10

From Relationship to Jail

I met a girl named Jalissa in December 1996 at the Otherside gay nightclub in Atlanta. I met her and another girl named Kay that same night. I was just leaning on the wall people watching. I had not been out since breaking up with Evelyn or should I say since Evelyn broke up with me. Anyway, Kay had sent her friend over to me to ask me if I was with anyone. I told her friend I was not. So, Kay came over to me and we talked a minute for what it was worth because it was hard as hell to hear in the club. We decided to exchange numbers and talk later.

I don't remember exactly how I ended up on the dance floor with Jalissa. She pretended like I had met her before, and my dumb butt tried to remember but I acted like I did remember. (Now you know I had never met that girl before.) Later I eventually found out she was not who she told me she was. Jalissa was the name she gave me. We danced a while and then exchanged numbers. She claims that when she met me before she had misplaced my number.

I would end up talking to both Kay and Jalissa. Not one more than the other. I was getting closer to Jalissa because she was calling me all the time. After I met Kay, I think I saw her maybe once more that month. I remember inviting her over to my apartment Christmas Eve and she spent the night. I even bought her a gift from Kirkland's for Christmas. Nothing physical ever happened between us. Even when she spent the night I slept on the couch and I gave her my bed. We parted ways the next day because I had to go to work Christmas day.

After that, it was all about Jalissa. I can remember a phone conversation I was having with her while I was at work. Her brother called and she put him in on the line. I thought I heard him call her Aubree. I was saying to myself I just know that this is not the same Aubree that Evelyn and Piper had been talking about. Not the one who does credit card fraud and steals other people's identity. So, I just let it go.

Right before New Year's, I invited Jalissa over to my apartment and she basically never left even though she had her own apartment and a roommate. On New Year's we got together with a couple of her friends, Tina and Crystal. We spent New Year's Day 1998 at their place. This was the day Jalissa confessed that she was in fact Aubree, Piper's ex. She was the stuntress (as I would call her). That really hurt my heart because I knew she was trouble. Her confession sounded sincere so I made a go of it anyway. But the relationship did have its share of drama the entire time we were together.

I knew Aubree was still upset with Piper for breaking up with her and I was kind of upset with Evelyn for dumping me for Piper. I guess I stuck with Aubree for revenge and she kind of did the same with me. Aubree was still in love with Piper and I knew that. I really did not care. I knew I should not have maintained a relationship with Aubree because it could have led me into trouble; which it did.

By February 1998, we had a pretty good Valentine's Day. Then March rolled around and we were getting into messy phone conversations with Evelyn and Piper. I even filed a police report against Evelyn for harassing phone calls. Unbeknownst to me, Evelyn had a warrant out on Aubree for the same thing. This was before I even met Aubree. Evidently Aubree never went to court so they had a warrant out on her for failure to appear to a court date. That is probably why Aubree chose to drive my car all the time and basically move in with me. She knew she had a warrant.

Between the drama and working two jobs to make ends meet, Evelyn had the nerve to come to my job and tell my Police Chief I was stalking her. I was still working with the City of McDonough as a police officer and a firefighter. My boss pulled me into a meeting to discuss the allegation. I told them she was an ex and that I was not stalking her. After the meeting they sent me back to work. I don't think they believed her. I could not believe that Evelyn was trying to get me fired.

Remember I was working at Kirkland's during the day and McDonough Police department at night. This meant my sleep was very limited. One night I pulled over to take a break from patrolling and I fell asleep. Well, I got caught and videotaped by my supervisor. Instead of firing me they allowed me to resign. At least they gave me that option so it did not look bad on my records when I applied for other police jobs.

I kept working at Kirkland's until I was able to get hired with Clayton State University as a part-time police officer. What I did not know was that Evelyn was still on the prowl. She found out I was working at Clayton State University and ultimately sent a letter to that Chief of Police defaming my character. Next thing I know they were cutting back on officers so they let me go; last hired, first fired. I think I worked there about a month. Evelyn had sent the same letter to the surrounding police departments so that they would not hire me. I know this because a friend of mine told me. My friend was working with one of the neighboring police departments and she received the letter.

Evelyn really tried to ruin my career. I had already pretty much stopped dealing with her. I did not know at times that she would come by my house to see if Aubree was there. She only did it because of the warrant. Once I found out about the warrant, I tried telling Aubree to turn herself in but she would not.

One day, Aubree and I got ready to go somewhere. When I started backing up, I noticed the sheriff's cars pulling up behind me. I knew then that Aubree was busted. I also noticed Evelyn's car in the parking lot. I had no idea how she knew where I was living. I guess she was staking out my place. After all, she was not working so she did not have anything else to do. The deputies, Aubree and myself went back into my apartment and I guess Aubree was trying to convince them that she was her twin sister. (She did have a twin, but they were not identical.) I just went into the bedroom and stayed while they talked to her in the living room.

The deputies knew I was not Aubree because I used to work with them. I could overhear Aubree asking them if she could talk to me. She came in the bedroom and asked me if she should tell them her real name and I told her yes. Aubree went back in the living room and let them take her into custody. After they left, I called Tina and Crystal and told them Aubree had been arrested. I asked them to come over because I was so emotional about everything. I did eventually go and get her out of jail that evening. After I got her out, she was given another court date and I had to make sure she showed up.

A few evenings later, Aubree showed me a picture of Piper wearing the ring that I had given Evelyn. I hit the roof. In April 1998, with Aubree's backing and insistence, I was determined to get the ring back somehow. Hell, I was not even finished paying for it. I then tried to ask for it back in a civil manner but Evelyn refused to give it back. My mother also tried because by this time she had taken over the payments. I could no longer make the payments.

I went to civil court to file a complaint against Evelyn. It was April 23, 1998 and I had asked Aubree not to come to court with me because she already had a pending case with Evelyn. When I got to court I thought I had all my evidence together but I guess I did not. I started off by telling the judge I was in a relationship with Evelyn for a couple of months. I told him I bought a ring that I let her wear because she said that she liked it. (I know that was not the real truth). Boy did that backfire. I really got caught up in my lie.

Evelyn brought her best friends to court with her. She really made me look like a fool in front of the judge and the deputies I used to work with from the sheriff's department. When Evelyn spoke, she told the judge I was harassing her and I gave her the ring. She also told the judge she was not in a relationship with me and I kept bothering her about being in one. She brought some of the hallmark cards I had given her throughout our short-lived relationship with her to court. One was the same card I put her $100 in for her phone bill that she had asked me for. I guess it was to try to show I was harassing her or stalking her. Now I understood why she used to give me cards and notes that were not signed by her. I was so stupid. She would just write something and not sign her name.

I can't even believe I still tried to help her even after she got fired from her job. This was even after she decided to see Aubree's ex-girlfriend. She also told the judge she did not ask for the ring. She said I gave her the ring along with a card. The judge believed her story over mine. I was trying to tell the judge the card was not for the ring; it was for the phone bill money she asked for. I told him Evelyn had asked me for the money to pay a bill because she lost her job. But the judge assumed it was the ring that was included with the card as a gift and not the $100.

The next thing I knew I was arrested in court, hand-cuffed and given a $20,000 bond. I don't think the bond would have been that high had not Evelyn told the judge I was a police officer. By this time, I had just started working with Stone Mountain Police Department. I had only been there three weeks. I had to look at Evelyn while I was being handcuffed and humiliated. I was charged with a felony (perjury) and faced the thought of losing my law enforcement certification. I just wanted to start crying right then and there.

I was placed with the other inmates who were there for court. After everyone's case was over, I walked down this long hallway to the holding cells and was placed inside one after I was pre-booked in. The first person I called was Aubree because she was at my house. She claimed she was going to try to get some money to get me out. But how? The chick was not working. She had been sitting her butt on my couch for the last couple of months wearing a dent in it. Then I called my mother and told her what happened because she knew I was going to court. She told me she could not help me and for me to call my father.

My dad said that he was going to try to get me out after he got off work. By this time, I was put back in my holding cell. While crying and looking out of the window,

I saw my Chief of Police from Stone Mountain pull up in the parking lot. I guess the jail called him since he was my boss. As soon as he came in, he held me and I started crying. He asked me was there anything he could do. He also told me that when I got out to report to him the following day. When he left, it was time for me to go to the actual jail and be processed in.

The women detention center was located in Forest Park Georgia. I had to ride in the van with about 5 other female inmates in handcuffs. Then instead of booking me in at Forest Park jail, they had a deputy escort me to Lovejoy jail in a patrol car to be booked in. It was so humiliating. I had co-workers scared to death to speak to me. At least I did not have to go in handcuffs from Forest Park to Lovejoy. Besides I had a handcuff key on me anyway. Not that I would have used it.

I had really messed up and I had to pay the price. When my dad got off work, he came to bond me out. I knew he did not have the money so he put his home up as a property bond. When I got in the car with him, I could not even look at him. He had to drive me back to the courthouse to get Aubree's car. When I got out of his car I told him I would call him later. My dad was there for me and I appreciate him a lot. I am and always will be daddy's little girl. When I got home, I got no love from Aubree. She sat her butt on that phone the whole night. She did not give a rat's behind about me. I went to my room with my dogs Precious and Champ and went to sleep.

The next day I had to report to work. The Chief let me go back to work for about three days but the mayor told him to suspend me until further notice because of my arrest. About a week later it was time for Aubree to go to court on her case with Evelyn. We went to court and I went with her as a witness. I had just got arrested for perjury. Wow. What the hell was I thinking?

The case went on and I did not testify too much because as soon as the prosecuting attorney asked me about my arrest for perjury I was excused from testifying. Aubree was found guilty and given probation. Now that all that was over it was time for me to find another job since I was suspended without pay.

A friend of mine from Hillman had a security company that she hired me for. It paid $15 an hour. I was working security at Club Nikki and Gentleman Club (both strip clubs) in Atlanta from 10:00 pm – 4:00 am two nights a week. I had also got a temporary job working from 7:00 am – 3:00 pm Monday through Friday. The day job did not last long because I was being late too much from oversleeping. So, all I had was the clubs to pay the rent which meant I was making $180 a week.

Every now and then Aubree would bounce one of her checks to pay a utility bill. She was still not working. By this time our relationship really was not a relationship. She was just living with me. I really wanted to tell her to leave but I think I was afraid to be alone. But then again, I also thought she would try to get me in trouble like Evelyn tried to do by making it seem like I was part of her illegal dealings. I can remember a time when she stole gas in my car because she drove off with the nozzle still hanging from my car. I was just hoping they did not get my tag number. I can also remember when Aubree got a new SUV (so I thought) and we drove the car to Louisiana. What I did not know was that she was supposed to return the car to the dealer. What she did was return the car, went back later and picked it up with the extra key she had found in the glove box when she first had the car. I was riding in and driving a stolen car. God must have been watching over me.

Aubree said she was an animal lover. She simply loved Precious. I don't think she cared for Champ. She would clearly show Precious more attention and affection. Champ was older and he had started losing some of his hearing. I could let Precious out without a leash and she would go out and come back on her own. I had to keep Champ on a leash because he could not hear me calling him. On several occasions I told Aubree not to let Champ out without having him on a leash. But did she listen? No.

Champ went missing for two days and she really did not care. I was crying my eyes out. Finally, a neighbor brought him back. The neighbor had been taking care of him and knew he belonged to me. I always wondered why the neighbor waited two days to return him. Maybe he saw Aubree do something to him or saw her put Champ out and let him roam. Maybe the neighbor wanted to make sure I was the one he returned Champ to instead of Aubree. I was just so happy to get him back but I am sure Aubree was pissed off.

By now I was able to go back to Hillman College and get a job even after my arrest because I left the first time in good standings. By this time, Sgt. Smith was no longer there. I would go to work and Aubree would still sit on her butt. At least she was there for my dogs. But the day I finally had the nerve to tell her she had to leave was a day I will never forget.

I had gotten ready to go to work at Hillman but I forgot my OC spray at the apartment. When I arrived at the apartment, I could hear Aubree fussing at Champ. The way the apartment was set up was you walk into the living room and kitchen. On the side of the kitchen there was a washer/dryer room. I guess Aubree did not hear me come in. I went toward the laundry room and I see Champ balled up in the corner and Aubree holding a belt over him. I wanted to punch her in the face but I was already out on bond. I asked her what the hell she was doing and she told me that Champ snapped at her. I said to myself he probably snapped at your butt because you have been beating on him when I am not home. That night I took Champ to work with me and left him in the car. She liked Precious so I knew she would not harm her while I was gone. After all my bosses left, I brought him in the office with me and kept him under the desk because I was dispatching that night. That night I told Aubree she had to go. She had given up her apartment a few months earlier but I did not care. I even had to give her money to move. I asked a friend for the money just to get her out my place and life.

After Aubree left, I remained friends with Tina and Crystal. I was more so friends with Crystal. We were just cool like that. I think Tina was jealous of me. To Crystal I was the perfect mate but there was no attraction between us. I could not disrespect their relationship like that. But I felt Tina did not care for me.

I had been single for a while and Crystal was trying to hook me up with a friend of hers. Her friend had been in a very abusive relationship with her girlfriend. Both physically and verbally. Crystal thought her friend should have gotten out of that unhealthy relationship. She thought I would be good for her.

I started talking to her on the phone and she finally came to meet me at my job at Hillman College. I thought she was attractive. We seemed to have a mutual attraction. But I also knew she had a crazy girlfriend so I was skeptical at first to even deal with her. She kept going back and forth with her girlfriend. They would have a physical fight and then she would let her apologize and take her back until the next fight. I guess she liked me enough to try to stay away from her girlfriend sometimes. We started dating and hanging out with Tina and Crystal on occasions.

The dating did not last long because she was having constant drama with her ex-girlfriend. I remember one night I had to be at work the next morning so I had gone to bed early. I got a call from her. She asked if she could come over because she just had a physical altercation with her ex-girlfriend to the point where the police had to be called. I told her sure no problem. When she got there she told me about the fight. She then showed me several marks on her back from being scratched with a set of keys. I tended to her scratches and told her to go to bed and get some rest. I gave her my bed and I went into the living room and slept on the couch. She left that next morning and went back home. At that point I thought it was best for us to just be friends and eventually the calls became few. The last time I did talk to her she was back with her ex-girlfriend.

While I was working at Hillman College, I used to hang out with and go to clubs with another co-worker named Vivian. At the time, the club to go to was called the Marquette. It was a sleazy hole in the wall club. It was a gay club that had horrible strippers, male and females, and they only sold Cisco and beer. They did have some great lip-syncing shows and female impersonators. That was the main reason I would go.

My friend Vivian had just broken up with her girl-friend of about 5 years. She was on the prowl that night. I had previously gotten out of a rough relationship with Aubree. I pretty much just went there to drink and get my mind off of her. While there, Vivian found a woman to keep her company. I was approached by a young girl who was flirting with me. She ended up being a 22-year-old Hillman student named Camille. Why me?

We exchanged phone numbers and went our separate ways for the rest of the night. I had gotten so inebriated that night. When we left the club, I fell asleep in the backseat of Vivian's car. I don't think she realized I had six beers. After Vivian dropped me off at my car, I did something stupid and that was get behind the wheel and try to drive home. I tried so hard to focus on getting myself home. It was a 20-minute drive.

About halfway there I had to pull over on the highway and throw up. I felt so bad. Then when I got to the entrance of my complex, I threw up again. My head was spinning the rest of the night. I said I would never do that again.

Now back to Camille. We tried to get to know each other but I knew it was not going to work because she was so young and I should not have tried to date another student. I was fine with just being friends. Every now and then after that she would drop by the Hillman office just to say hello. By this time school was letting out for the summer.

When school started back up, we hired another Black female. She was gay also. We became friends. We were both trying to find the love of our lives. At one point I had placed a personal ad in an Atlanta paper called "creative loafing". I had several responses. One response came from a woman named Carol. Carol was 6'1". I knew she was too tall for me but I thought I would try going out with her anyway. We spoke on the phone several times and she came to meet me at my job. When she pulled up, she had on a lot of make-up but she was pretty. We had a few dates, but it did not last long either. She was too tall for me. I looked funny standing next to her with me being 5'7".

Like the other women I dated, I just ended it with us being friends until we eventually stopped contacting each other. I met another woman named Paula. Paula did the same and came to meet me at my job. She was totally opposite. She was about 5'0". She was pretty but she was not my type. We just left it at being friends. After Paula, I stopped with the ads and just kept to myself. This was around the time I started concentrating on writing poetry. Vivian wrote poetry so she kind of inspired me to write. I was about to stop dealing with women all together but I could not bear the thought of being in a relationship with a man. I knew I would only be doing it because society says it is normal. So, I guess I would be considered not normal in the eyes of society.

I was not willing to live an uncomfortable life for the sake of society. I did not get any enjoyment in being intimate with or having a life with a man. In my lifetime, I had slept with six men. It was mostly sex. The sexual assault in the military really made me not want to be in a relationship with one. Maybe that is the reason why I completely chose to be gay. I will never know and I have already stopped trying to figure it out. Some people say they are born gay and some say it is a choice. I am not sure which category I fall in.

Samgrelletta Z. Fairley

CHAPTER 11

Georgia Regional

When I was working for Stone Mountain Police Department, I worked with a guy named Adrian. Adrian also worked at Georgia Regional Hospital as a police officer. He spoke to his Chief about me when he learned I had lost my job. I did not have much faith about getting another job in law enforcement but I had an opportunity to get an interview. At that time, I felt my life was so complex. I kept my emotions silent.

During my interview, I had no problem telling the Chief about my situation but I did not tell her about my lifestyle. I was very honest with her when it came to my arrest. She knew I was pending a felony charge. I don't know what made her do it but she gave me the job. I was the only female police officer at the department. Maybe she saw something in me that I did not see in myself.

While working there I had to continue to go to court every month for about a year. My case kept getting postponed. I was at least glad I had an attorney. My dad was there to help me pay for the attorney. I think it made him more comfortable to know that I had an attorney. When I finally had my case heard by a judge, my attorney was able to get my felony charges reduced to a misdemeanor charge and I was given probation for 12 months. The judge allowed me to plead the Georgia First Offender Act which meant that once my probation was over it would be as if I did not have an arrest record. My record could not be used against me. I had finally gotten that part of my life over with after a year of worry. I was no longer in jeopardy of losing my law enforcement certification. My attorney was very sloppy but he did his job. I don't even think I finished paying him nor did he come after me for the rest of his money. I guess he knew I really could not afford it. He saved my career.

I was extremely happy to tell the Chief that the case was over. During that time in my life, I had lost a lot of weight. After that saga, I had started gaining my weight back. It was a very stressful time. I was barely making ends meet so I would only eat bologna sandwiches and noodles. My dogs would eat milk bones. I did not like asking people for help or money so I made do.

Chief gave me a second chance at having a law enforcement career. The money was not much but it paid the bills. I was also still working with Hillman College part time. At Georgia Regional I was more experienced than most of the other officers. A lot of them had animosity toward me because of it; however, for the most part, everyone at Georgia Regional got along like a family. We had parties for birthdays and we had holiday dinners together. Chief and I did clash sometimes but we still had respect for each other. The same goes for the Lieutenant of the department. The department was so small that everyone always wanted to be in everyone else's business.

After about a year I was talked into taking a test for a Sergeant position. I just knew she was going to give it to someone who had been there longer but it was determined that I had scored the highest amongst the others who took the test. I was now the day watch Sergeant. After I became Sergeant, I noticed our officers had not been to the firing range and it is required by the State that you must qualify every year. Since I had a good repour with my chief at Hillman, he allowed my officers to participate in qualifying at the range alongside Hillman officers.

I usually scored in the low 90s; however, I must admit my officers did terribly at the range. It was very embarrassing. Hillman Chief did everything he could possibly do to help them qualify. After that they were not allowed to carry a weapon until they found a place on their own to qualify. It was okay not to carry a weapon at the hospital. The hospital was a mental hospital. We were not allowed to carry weapons inside the buildings.

I did not go into any of the buildings unless we were called by staff. Every now and then I would go in the gym and if any of the patients were in there, I would play basketball with them so they would have a good trust factor in us as officers. Even though we very seldom received a lot of unruly patient calls; I experienced two. Both calls involved the same female who was a regular patient with the facility. The first call came from Intake. She had become very unruly and would not listen to the staff. When I arrived and saw her, she had taken all her clothes off. Since I knew her, I tried to talk to her and try to get her to put her clothes back on. She would talk back to me but she was not trying to put her clothes back on.

After I requested for another officer to respond, both of us were in an open-door room with telephones on a counter. I was trying to keep her confined to the room so that she was not out in the open naked. I guess at some point she was getting tired of talking and wanted to leave the room. When she attempted to leave I tried to grab her arm and hold her back. Considering I was about 120 lbs.

and she was 200 lbs., that was not working out the way I planned. So, then I tried to grab her whole body from behind. That did not work either.

While I was still holding on, she started knocking the phones off the counter. I was being slung back and forth like a rag doll. Did I tell you she was naked? Finally, my other officer came and we were able to handcuff her and get a blanket to put over her. After all of that she finally calmed down and we were able to get her to put her clothes on and she became very cooperative with the Intake personnel.

The second incident involved the same female. This time she was in her assigned room and had broken the glass in a picture frame in her room. Now the glass in all the pictures were supposed to be non-breakable. When I got to the room, one of the counselors were trying to talk to her. She was holding a piece of glass to her neck that she had gotten from the broken picture. The staff thought it would be best to use a mattress to pin her up against the wall when she was not looking in hopes she would drop the piece of glass. So, while a counselor was talking to her, we were prepared to catch her off guard. The more we tried to move in, the more she kept sticking the glass to her neck.

All of a sudden, another counselor who was familiar with her came in and started talking to her. She started focusing her attention on him and commented on the yellow shirt he was wearing. It was because of the yellow shirt that the counselor was able to get the piece of glass from her. She calmed down after that.

I really enjoyed my time at Georgia Regional and I really appreciated the Chief understanding my situation and giving me a second chance at being a police officer. I was also good friends with a female who worked in the building next to mine (Mitzi). This was also the time when I was introduced to a woman named Amy. Amy worked with Mitzi. I had never seen her before until I had to go to the personnel building. I remember when she came out of her office but I really did not give her a second look.

It was Mitzi who told me she wanted to meet me. Mitzi knew I was gay. I told Mitzi to give her my number and tell her to call me. She ended up calling me while I was at work. I think it was around a holiday (July 4th) in which she was off that day. I remember telling her to bring me some bar-b-que. She said she would. I can't remember if she did or not.

I eventually invited her over to my place one night. She looked totally different. She was cute. She had a slim body and a fitted long skirt with a strap shirt. Her hair was long and wrapped. She was meeting up with some of her friends that evening so she decided to stop by beforehand. We messed around but nothing serious and then she left.

After that we kind of started dating. I was always dating after the first visit. That was one of my problems. I kept going from one relationship to another and not spending time with myself.

After about a month, my co-workers started getting nosey because I started driving Amy's car to work sometimes. It had gotten to the point where even Chief noticed and was trying to hint to us not to date other employees of the hospital. I think someone told her about me and Amy. I always felt like the Chief already knew about my lifestyle anyway.

One thing about her, she would not hire another female. But when one of our officers left, she finally decided to. This was around the time I was trying to get another job. I think she did that because she always wanted to have a female officer on staff. The female lasted just long enough for Chief to get rid of her. The officer had a drinking problem and had gotten arrested for driving under the influence (DUI).

Now back to my relationship with Amy. Amy was a sweet person. Amy had a bachelor's degree and a master's degree. When I met her, she was trying to get into medical school but was not having any luck. I told Amy I would do what I could to help her get into medical school. I spent a lot of time at her apartment even though she had a roommate. I spent about two nights a week at her place. I never understood why she did not want to spend more time at my place since I did not have a roommate.

The first couple of month's things were good between us. When the holidays started coming around, she started to withdraw from me. I tried to be understanding because in between her working, playing sports, and writing papers to get into med school, I knew she was going through a lot. I also knew Amy was young for me but she gave me companionship.

After applying for several medical schools, she finally got an interview. That process was not cheap. The application fees were at least $125 per application. She had several of them. I even paid for a couple of them trying to help her out. I did not make that much money but I did what I could to help.

One day Amy asked me to go somewhere with her but she said I would have to dress casually. At the time I did not know she wanted me to go to a house party at her aunt's home. I wore a fitted black shirt and some gray and black pants with some flat shoes. Yeah, I know it sounds corny but I was comfortable. Interestingly the whole time I was there I was very uncomfortable. I felt like I had to pretend to be straight around her family and friends. I knew people at the party were talking about me. I never hung around her family again after that.

Now it was time for Christmas and I mentioned to Amy that I wanted a Play Station game. Like I said I did not make that much money but I was still able to get Amy some CD's she wanted. When it was time for me to exchange gifts with Amy, I felt like a fool and wanted to crawl under a rock.

Amy gave me my gift first which was the Play Station game. I really was not expecting it. Then it was time for me to give her her gifts. I did not want to but I had to give her something. She had made a list and I had planned on getting most of her gifts my next pay period. I saw the look of disappointment on her face when I gave her the gift. Hell, I felt so bad I did not want to take her gift.

A week later we went to Alison's New Year's party. After the party I found myself pulling away from the relationship because Amy had become extremely distant from me. In February we went to a Valentine's Day party at Alison's. This was to be the last get together for us. I thought it was best for Amy and I to just be friends. I started limiting my calls to her and I stopped taking her out. The relationship was just not working anymore. Again, I had to realize she was too young for me.

By this time, Amy had transferred to another division which was located in downtown Atlanta. Finally, she called me one day and I just told her that I thought we should not talk or see each other anymore. Then she wanted to know why. I told her she did not know what she wanted in life and I was not the one to try to wait and see. I told her I wanted someone to grow old with and not someone who wanted me to be a certain way around her family. She started crying on the phone but I did not change my mind. We may have been together for about 8 months.

Now back at work. After I made Sergeant, I had to go to a supervisors training course for my new position. When I went to the class at Fulton County Police Academy, I met a female Lieutenant from Fulton County Police Department. She convinced me to apply with Fulton County because they needed female officers. I just knew I was not going to get hired and I really did not want to waste the paperwork and the Lieutenant's time. Still, somehow, I just tried for the hell of it.

After I filled out the application and turned it in, I received a test date for the police exam. I went to take the test and according to the Lieutenant, I did okay. My next step was to complete a stack of paperwork. It was a booklet of information that needed to be filled out about my background. After I turned that in to the Lieutenant, I just knew it was going to be turned down. I was very honest about everything including my arrest two years prior. I had no reason to lie.

About a month had gone by and I had not heard anything from the Lieutenant so I assumed it was not approved. Then one day when I checked my phone messages, I received a message from the Lieutenant asking me to give her a call. When I called her back, she asked me if I would be able to come and go through the physical agility test and I said sure. I was able to pass the test even though I was out of shape. The following week she scheduled me for a physical and I passed with flying colors. A couple of weeks later, I was scheduled for a polygraph and passed it as well.

After that I guess she had to do the finishing touches on my background. I had passed all stages of the hiring process. Now it was time for a final interview in front of a panel. I was very nervous. I had my friend Monica from Georgia Regional help me pick out some shoes for my one interview suit. She was the Chief's secretary and a good friend of mine.

I had my skirt outfit ready to go. I had to go to my interview while I was at work at Georgia Regional. When I arrived, there was another applicant in front of me. The Lieutenant told me I would find out after the interview if I was going to be hired or not. I was praying hard about that one. I went in and I made eye contact with each individual who asked me a question. I wanted them to know I was attentive and confident. Once the interview was over, I stepped out for a second and waited in another room.

The Lieutenant came out and asked me how I felt about the interview. I told her I was nervous but I was glad it was over. She said she told me it was not going to be bad and then she asked me when could I start. My mouth just dropped. I told her I must give a normal two weeks notice plus a week to handle personal business. I just really wanted some time off in between jobs. We calculated it and came up with a start date of April 24, 2000.

I left and went back to work so damn happy. The county had decided to take a chance on me. I hated to leave Chief because without her I would not have been able to apply with Fulton County. Not only would I have to resign from Georgia Regional but I would also have to resign from Hillman Police Department. I would not be able to continue working at those departments while I was working for Fulton County.

In the meantime, I met a woman named Morgan. Morgan was single and lived in Albany. She was also in the military. I started getting to know her through the Internet; and we seemed to have a lot in common. It had gotten to the point where I could not wait to hear from her and I looked forward to her emails. I sent her a picture of me and she said she liked it. She sent me a picture of her and her boys. My first impression was that she was kind of a plain Jane.

While talking to her on the phone, she said she was on her way to see me and I said yeah right. I played her little game and gave her directions. I was actually at work at Georgia Regional on this day. It was a weekend and I usally stayed in the office unless I got a call. As soon as I went to the front gate to relieve my co-worker, she pulled up. She was 5'2" and about 120lbs. She was kind of cuter in person.

Well, she stayed with me the rest of my shift. We hung out in my office. I gave her a hug and then a kiss. After she left we decided to start dating. We lived a couple of hours away from each other so we kept talking on the phone and sending emails. Morgan was a good support system for me at the time. I told her about all my mishaps. She would always tell me I was very intelligent and that I could do anything I put my mind to.

Before I started working with Fulton County Police Department, I took a week off and spent that time with Morgan and her boys in Albany. Prior to me going, I started talking to her boys on the phone so they could get to know me before I just popped up at their home. They were very mannerable. I had also taken my babies Precious and Champ.

The boys and Morgan loved my dogs. The oldest son would get Precious and the youngest son would get Champ. I really thought Morgan was the one. I even told my mother Morgan was a very responsible woman and financially secure. I tried to tell her about some of the women in my life but I don't think she really wanted to hear it. She just wanted to know where I would be when I would go out of town. I don't think she really wanted to hear about anything dealing with my lifestyle.

CHAPTER 12

Out of Control

When I started working for Fulton County, I had to be in training for 6 weeks. While I was in training, I had the weekends off so I would go see Morgan and the boys. Most of my training officers were okay. There were only two other Black females at the department. One was gay (Heather) and the other I could not tell if she was or not. I ended up riding on patrol with Heather. I was not sure about her until one of my training officers said that she date girls. So, for that shift we ended up learning that both of us were gay and that we knew some of the same people. I told her I was dating Morgan and I even wore a ring that Morgan gave me.

At the time she was just dating different women and was not in a relationship. She would also talk about her cousin alot. On Wednesdays we started hanging out at the clubs. I told Morgan I had found a friend to hang out with.

I had not hung out like that in a while. It was fun. But I still respected Morgan. I may have looked at other women but that was it.

Heather and I almost went out every Wednesday. I think it was then that I began to have second thoughts about being in a relationship. I knew Morgan was not that feminine on the outside but she was on the inside. I like feminine aggressive women. I started seeing so many feminine women in the clubs. It had come to a point where the visit to Albany became far and few. After things started changing, Morgan starting calling me all the time even after I told her I was going out. She would call me back-to-back and I did not like that at all. If I don't answer, give me an opportunity to call you back. It was never anything important she had to say. I was wrong and I know it but I did not care at the time. I wanted to do what I wanted to do and have my cake to.

Now it was time for me to be released from training which meant that I got to ride by myself in my patrol car. It was a good day that day. I considered myself the real police. It would soon be short lived. About three weeks after I was released from training, I was given a letter placing me on administrative leave. I had to work in the office until further notice. One of the Deputy Chiefs said something came up in my background. I just think that was their way of trying not to hire another Black female. I just prayed every day while working in the office and hoped I would not be let go. But just in case, I started looking for other employment. I even took the Postal exam.

After a few weeks, it was time to go before the Chief of Police, Deputy Chief and my Major to determine if I was to stay employed with Fulton County. The chief was sitting in front of me and the others were sitting behind me. I was scared to death. Chief gave me a lecture. I really did not have anything to say because I thought I was totally honest about my background including my arrest. I think it was the Deputy Chief who really did not want me to stay. But when the Chief said he would give me an opportunity to stay employed with the county I was very happy. I was now able to go back to the streets and work extra-jobs. I am sure the other people did not agree with that but I know that I am a good officer and all I needed was a second chance.

During this time, I was getting more distant from Morgan. I knew Morgan had gotten an assignment to Texas and would be leaving soon and I really did not want to be in a long-distance relationship. Since going out with Heather I was having a lot of fun. On one of our club outings, Heather had invited her cousin Monica up from Perry, Georgia. When I met her, there was an instant attraction on both our parts.

It was very crowded in the club so I went with Monica to the restroom to stand by the door because half of them did not lock. We went back to the dance floor and we kind of started dancing in place. Next thing I know I just looked back at Monica and then we kissed. After that I really started pulling away from Morgan and started concentrating on Monica. After Morgan moved to Texas, I started going to Perry to visit Monica. She had decided that she wanted to relocate to Atlanta.

She started coming to Atlanta for job interviews. Once she obtained a job she moved up and stayed with me for a couple of months to save money. When she did move, she ended up moving around the corner from me. During this time, I was becoming friends with one of our dispatchers named Laura.

Laura was from New York and I used to tease her about her accent. I thought it was cute. Laura was married with children. Her husband was also in law enforcement but with a different department. We started talking more through the in-car computer in the patrol car. Later we decided to exchange numbers. We talked for about two months before we even met.

One day I had a class at our headquarters building and during my lunch I decided to go meet Laura. While I was waiting for her to come back from lunch, I noticed a picture of her outside the offices. I thought she was a cute woman. So when she came in, I knew who she was, but she did not know me. After we met, we started hanging out a little at her house. Her husband had a pool table and I would go over and play pool with them. I did not care for her husband because he would make fun of her size in front of other people and thought it was funny. I did not like that at all. I found out through Laura that he always teased her about her size.

At first, I think I scared Laura when I first called her and asked her to hang out. She thought I was trying to date her. I just wanted a cool friend. Now Monica did not care for me talking to Laura because she thought something was strange about the whole situation. I was really looking for people to hang with—nothing more and that included Laura.

I had a few girlfriends dictate who I could and couldn't talk to and I was not going to allow Monica to do the same to me. So I kept talking to Laura and I would hang out with her, at least while Monica was at work. I would make sure I was home before she got off. Monica was still living with me at this time. I know it was wrong to sneak around but again I did not care.

As the weeks went by, I started catching feelings for Laura but I would not say anything. I would talk to her as soon as I woke up and I would talk to her just before Monica would get home. I was doing it on the down low. What I did not know was that she was catching feelings for me also. Meanwhile I was not happy with Monica because I did not like her telling me who I could and could not talk to and not to mention my feelings was detouring elsewhere. I never had any intentions on catching feelings for Laura it just happened. I think we both got tired of certain aspects within our relationships. One thing led to another and we eventually told each other how we felt.

Now we were both doing things on the down low. I would soon start going over to her house when her husband was at work but we never had any physical contact other than a hug. It came down to a point of us meeting almost every day after work in a parking lot to talk. That was how we ended our day.

Now it was time for something more serious and that was an intimate experience. I think the first time was difficult for the both of us. I went to her house, again while her husband was at work, and we were intimate. I was very bold doing that in her home. After that experience we started going to a hotel for our escapades. Yes, we were cheating on our mates. Yes, I was sleeping with Laura and she was still married and sleeping with her husband. I was not sleeping with Monica because I was trying to get out of the relationship.

Once Monica moved, Laura would come over before she went to work. This lasted for about two months. One month prior, Monica and I had finally broken up. But I do remember one-night Monica came to my house and tried to get me to start a fight. I kept trying to close my door but she kept putting her foot in it preventing it from closing all the way. This night I had a radio and my motorcycle battery on my porch. When she finally left, she took those items. I went and filed a police report with the Police Department but I did not name her as the one who took it. I told her cousin Heather about it and then my things were mysteriously returned while I was not at home.

I felt that Heather was involved in my relationship with her cousin a little too much. She was the reason Monica did not want me talking to Laura from the beginning because of something she said about Laura. But anyway, Laura's husband Cedric's birthday rolled around and she also had a friend from New York come and stay a few days. Cedric did not know about me and Laura at the time because I went to his birthday party. It was after that when stuff hit the fan and he found out some kind of way. He was calling her all kinds of names and in front of her daughter. He eventually moved out but he also convinced his daughter to move with him. That really devastated Laura.

This was around the time of the 2003 NBA All-Star game which was held in Atlanta. I knew Laura was going through things so I sent for her sister to come and spend a few days with her. She was so happy. I told her my uncle was coming and I had to pick him up from the airport. I was really picking up her sister. I pulled up at the airport curb and got out as if to meet my uncle and then her sister came around the car. Laura was so happy she cried.

After a while her daughter started wanting Laura to come spend the night with her at her dad's place when he would work the night shift and she agreed. I trusted Laura to go and be with her daughter and not deal with her husband.

As the months went by her daughter had started coming back to Laura's house to spend the weekends with her. I never went around because I knew how her daughter felt about me. Laura and I's relationship was still going stronger than ever. She had even told her mother about us. Her mother was a minister and I was kind of scared about that.

One weekend her son came through Atlanta for the weekend from school. She wanted me to meet him so I told her to bring him to the gym where I was playing basketball. I met her son at a place called Run and Shoot. I guess he knew I was gay because he told Laura she better not be messing with me. After a while I would spend more time at Laura's house with my dogs. She had a backyard and it was easier to just let them outside and me not have to walk them. Me and her daughter had started speaking again by this point. She also did not mind my dogs being around. But there were still times when Laura would go and spend the night with her daughter at her dad's place. I must admit I was a little scared they might have sex because after all I was Laura's first female relationship and he was her husband of 17 years.

After her husband moved, he would not come over to the house unannounced because he did not want to cross paths with me. One day he did come unannounced while Laura and I were at work. By this time, I was practically staying with Laura even though I had my own place and my dogs would stay in the basement when we were not home. That man turned my life upside down when he came in the house and killed my dog.

CHAPTER 13

Precious and Champ

Since her husband had finally moved out on February 10, 2003 I had pretty much starting staying with Laura to try to help her maintain her sanity since he took everything but the bedroom furniture, a sofa and loveseat. Laura and Cedric had an off again, on-again speaking arrangement. Some days he would be nice and some days he would call her all kinds of bad names.

Around the last week of March, Cedric was having car troubles. I guess he knew he should be nice to Laura because he would need a ride from dropping his car off for repairs. Laura was already feeling bad about breaking up her home so she still carried her same good person mentality. On March 30, 2003 Cedric needed a ride from the car repair shop. This was a weekend that Laura's daughter came to stay.

On March 31, 2003 Laura and I went to work while

her daughter was at the house with my dogs. They were such sweet dogs and very loveable. They would be so excited when someone would come downstairs and open the door so that someone would play with them. They would jump on you for attention. They were my kids. Precious was 10 and Champ was 12 years old. They had just gotten haircuts and were looking so cute.

On this day Cedric decided to go over to the house while Laura was not home claiming to look for something that he left in the basement. Now he had ample opportunity to get the rest of his things earlier but chose not to. He had already been gone for about 2 months and now suddenly he needed to look for something.

When Laura told me that he was going to the house, I told her he better not hurt my dogs. I knew Desiree was going to let him in because it was her father. Laura told me Cedric only stayed about five minutes because he claimed it was too much stuff to go through and my dogs were in the basement so he left. Now when he moved out, we had all the windows properly secured so no one could get in and Cedric no longer had a key. But there was one window in the basement that did not lock. I had placed a piece of wood in the window when Cedric moved out so that no one could slide the window open from the outside. It was a window near the ground that had bushes in front of it.

When I got home that evening, I checked on my dogs and they were fine but it did not don on me to check for anything else suspicious in the basement. I thought he just left because he got irritated. Well on April 1, 2003 Laura and I went to work and Desiree went to school. The alarm system was inoperable but could be set to at least make a beeping sound when anyone entered the house and only Cedric, Desiree, Laura and myself knew the code. The alarm was set when we all left the house. Later that evening I had to work an extra job at Home Depot and Laura had a training class after work. Desiree came home from school and deactivated the alarm. Desiree would always call her mother when she came home from school. This time Laura asked Desiree to feed and let my dogs out because we were coming home late and Desiree said, okay. Meanwhile I was at my extra job waiting on my parents to come do some shopping.

Before my parents got there, I received a call from Laura. She told me Desiree said something was wrong with my dogs. Desiree told Laura that Precious was not moving. Laura told Desiree to go see if she could see what was wrong and Desiree told her she was scared. Laura then told me she was leaving class early to go see what was wrong with my dogs. Meanwhile my parents arrived and I had to act like nothing was wrong. I was very concerned about what was going on with my dogs. I could not talk to Laura while my parents were there with me so I had to wait for them to leave.

By this time Laura was at the house and I called her. What she told me made my heart sink. Laura told me Precious had blood around her mouth and she was not moving or breathing. She also said that something was wrong with Champ. She said that when she called out to Champ he tried to get up but could not. She picked him up and took him upstairs with her and covered Precious with a sheet.

I left work and went home crying the whole way there. When I got there, I went directly downstairs. I looked through the door frame and saw a sheet lying on the floor. I had to get the nerve up to go in there and see what was wrong with my Precious. I went over to her and stood over her for a second because I was scared to take the sheet off of her. When I did get the nerve to remove the sheet, I just looked at Precious and cried. I was asking Precious to tell me who did that to her.

Precious had been with me since she was 8 weeks old. She was like my child and I got Champ when he was 5 years old. I looked at the blood around her mouth and head. I just bent over her and rubbed her. I went to get a box and I wrapped her in the sheet and left to take her to the vet. I did not speak to anyone in the house.

Laura called me while I was enroute to the vet and told me that she thinks something was wrong with Champ. I went back to get Laura and Champ. When I put Champ in the back seat, he started howling from being in pain. I did not know what was wrong with him. I knew Precious was dead. I did not say anything to Laura while we were in the car. I got to the vet and the first thing they asked me was if there was any poison in the house. They thought Precious was poisoned. They took Champ in the back for x-rays.

By this time, I had to call my parents. They came to the veterinarian and I had to tell them what happened to my babies. I decided to send Precious away for an autopsy. I wanted to know exactly what happened to her. It cost about $400 that I did not have but I made a way to pay for it. I just could not believe my Precious was gone. All I remember is all that blood. The doctor came out and told me what was wrong with Champ. She told me Champ had two dislocated hips. She said that it was as if someone held him up by his hind legs and just snapped them out of place. He said they could operate but it was not an assurance that he would be normal after the surgery. I told them to go ahead and try then I would at least still have him.

The rest of that night my parents were telling me to

come home and get out of that situation because they feared for my life but I loved Laura so much I could not bear the thought of leaving her by herself. Eventually I did leave for a couple of days. I told my parents I thought that when Cedric came over on March 31, 2003, he moved the piece of wood that I had in the window and it went unnoticed by me. I thought Cedric came over while everyone was gone on April 1, 2003. It would not have looked suspicious to anyone to see his car there because he used to live there.

I think Cedric came in, cut the alarm off, killed my dogs, put the wood back, reset the alarm and left my dogs to die. Even though the alarm was not activated through the alarm company, there was a way to be able to tell if someone was in a censored area. That day, Cedric was in the basement area. I was on guard after that to the point of carrying my weapon with me everywhere I went. I later found out Cedric knew where I lived and how to get there. He had written my address on one of his business cards. It was given to me by Laura when she found it in some of his things.

On April 2, 2003 I had class at the police academy. That morning the vet called my residence and spoke with my mother. My mother then called me and told me to call the vet because they said that Champ would not survive the surgery. His spine was badly damaged as well. So that morning I cried and called them back. The vet explained to me that the best thing to do was to have him put to sleep. I had agreed because I did not want him in any unnecessary pain. I had asked the vet not to do anything until I could come and be with him one last time.

I went to see Champ for the last time after my class. Laura met me there. I went to the back where Champ was laying. He was still hooked up to an IV. His eyes were closed, and he had a jerking motion in his body. I just stood there rubbing on him. We both started crying. Laura then stood back but I kept rubbing him. Suddenly Champ opened his eyes. I was so happy because he could now see me, his mom. He was trying to raise up as if he wanted me to pick him up or he was trying to tell me something but he was in so much pain it was hard for him. I kept rubbing him and kissing on him so he could feel my love.

I asked the doctor how long the process would take. She said that it would take about 10 seconds. I just kept rubbing on him and he kept trying to look up at me. Then I guess the pain became too unbearable for him and he started whining and hollering in pain. I started crying more but I kept rubbing him the whole time. I finally told the doctor that I was ready to let him go.

The doctor then took a needle with liquid in it and put it through the IV tube in his leg. Within 10 seconds Champ close his eyes for the last time and he was gone. I continued to rub him some more. I then kissed him good-bye. I took his dog collar from his neck and I walked away. I also took Precious' dog collar as well. I started hanging them from my rearview mirror in my car. I was so mad I just wanted to hurt Cedric for doing that to my dogs. Did I see him do it, did I have proof that he did it, no. I just knew he killed my dogs.

A few days later I went to the local police station to file a cruelty to animal report against Cedric. I remember explaining my situation to the desk sergeant and why I thought Cedric did it. Like any other police station it was good and funny humor because I told them I thought my girlfriend's husband killed my dogs. I can tell they did not want to do the report so they sent me to animal control.

I did what they said but animal control said that the police department will do the report for cruelty to animals. I spoke to the detective over my case and he came out to the house to see the area. I don't think he was very interested in the case because it was not a first on his list. He did say he thought Cedric did do it based on the situation. I was prepared to have Cedric charged with felony cruelty to animals but Laura did not want me to.

We really did not know if Cedric was going to kill us next or what. We tried to get a restraining order against him but when we got to court Cedric tried to humiliate Laura and myself. He only spoke about everything that dealt with my relationship with Laura. The judge even asked him did he kill my dogs, as if it was a joke. But I knew it was not going to work because we were in Cedric's territory, meaning he was a police officer for the same jurisdiction where we were in court. We never got the restraining order.

I just thought it was interesting that on March 30, 2003 Cedric was talking to Laura because he needed a ride, then on March 31, 2003, he was pissed off again and then April 1, 2003 my dogs were killed. We never heard from Cedric after that. Not even for a ride to go pick up his vehicle when it was finished being repaired.

After a couple of days, I received a call from the vet around midnight. I guess she could not wait to tell me the results of Precious' autopsy. When she started reading what the autopsy said, I just started crying again. She said Precious' skull was crushed. She said it was caused by blunt force trauma, meaning someone use a blunt object and repeatedly struck Precious in the head. That was the blood that was in her mouth. She had hemorrhaged.

At that point, all I could think of was doing something to Cedric because I thought he used his police baton and beat my dog with it. I pictured him coming downstairs and opening the door to where my dogs were. Knowing them, they thought the person who opened the door was friendly and they probably jumped on him thinking they could get rubbed. But instead, he struck them with his asp baton. He just left them there to suffer and die.

I called Laura that same night and just repeated that I was going to get Cedric. I was not going to physically harm him in anyway but I was going to try to ruin his career. But for some reason, Laura still did not want me to do anything to him. She agreed about the police report but she did not want me to do anything else to him. I was trying to figure out why. Did she still want to be with this man? I was so confused. I was trying to figure out why she was protecting him.

Her thing was if I caused him to lose his job then he would lose his apartment and maybe his vehicle. He had already lost his wife and she thought that would push him over the edge. But I did not give a damn about him losing nothing. He could have messed up my car or something. He did not have to kill my dogs.

For the next few weeks, my head was hurting so bad. After I went to the doctor they told to me that my blood pressure was up 150 over 110. I assumed that was not good. But the pressure of losing my dogs like that and stressing over watching my back everywhere I went was getting to be a bit much for me. I tried to calm down but I was still out to get Cedric. I had prepared a letter to send to his Chief of Police but again Laura did not want me to do it. It had gotten to the point where I just left it alone altogether. I never heard from the detective over my case. I guess it was not even important to them to give me a courtesy call and just say the case was closed because no one saw him do it.

I don't even know how he could live with himself. I don't know what I would do if I encountered Cedric. I know it would bring hatred even though I am supposed to forgive him according to God. It is so hard to forgive that man. I even tried to put myself in his shoes with his situation of losing Laura but I did not kill his daughter. Maybe it's not fair to compare a human life to a dog's life but to me my dogs were human and they were my life.

For the next several months, I had my crying moments about the situation. I tried to maintain my sanity but every now and then I shed tears because I miss them. They were there with me when no one else was. They listened to me and loved me unconditionally. They were there when I only had noodles and bologna to eat because I had to pay other bills after being arrested. They were there eating just milk bones for dinner because that was all I could afford. They were always there but now I know they are resting in puppy paradise. They had crossed over rainbow bridge and they were together. It was hard to get back to work after that but I knew I had too.

Now back to work. I did enjoy working for the police department. Several cases are so rememberable. I remember responding to a car fire. The driver had driven up the side of an exit ramp and struck an overpass bridge. The vehicle immediately burst into flames. The driver was unable to get out of the vehicle. After the fire department put the flames out, I could see the driver still in a seated position but completely non-recognizable.

I also responded to several suicides. One person jumped from a 4th-floor balcony and was decapitated by striking a lower balcony railing. The other person jumped from a parking garage. This was the first time I actually saw brain matter. In my career as a police officer, I think I have seen it all. My most memorable moment was when I captured a murder suspect without back-up. I can honestly say that none of my days were ever the same.

When Mother's Day came around, I was able to send Laura to New York to spend time with her mother. By July, my father was getting ready to move to Mississippi. When my dad sold his house, he had moved in with me until he could retire. He lived with me for about 8 months. I spent most of my time at Laura's when he did move in. I know I should have spent more time with my dad. I regret that I was thinking of myself instead of spending more quality time with my dad who had been there for me through everything. I must say that I hated to see him go even though I was not there most of the time.

Meanwhile Desiree was speaking to me off and on again. She started really speaking to me after her father killed my dogs. I think she knew her father did it. I guess she felt sorry for me but I could not dismiss the fact that she still turned her back on her mother and moved in with her father. But it was okay, I guess.

CHAPTER 14

New York

We had been planning this trip for months, working hard and saving money. The day came for us to go to the airport. I was excited but also scared because I was going to meet her family for the first time. Even though I had spoken with everyone on the phone, I was still nervous. Especially with meeting her mother, the minister.

We had everything packed the night before. I had a restless night because I was excited. Our flight was scheduled to leave around 6:00 pm that evening. Earlier we had called to try to get an earlier flight because I had taken the day off at the last minute and it would have gotten us there before dark. We were able to change the flight to leave around 5:00 pm. We called for a cab. Our driver was a hispanic lady and a pregnant Black female riding shotgun. The pregnant female was reading some article about sex and then a conversation started about circumcision. Now you know I could care less but they were truly funny.

When we got to the airport, we noticed the flight had been delayed 30 minutes due to the weather in New York—heavy rainstorms. Then it was delayed another 30 minutes. It was delayed back to our original time so I called the airport to get a credit which they did give me. Then they canceled the flight altogether. We called Laura's mother and told he her we could not get out until the next day. We were now stuck at the airport.

The airlines offered to put people up in a hotel so we said cool and they had a shuttle to transport people. I did not know that the voucher for the room would have to come out of our pockets. They said they don't pay when a cancellation is due to weather so we decided to call a friend from work. She took us back to the condo because it was close to the airport. She even offered to take us back to the airport the next day.

The next day we headed back to the airport. I thought my luggage was going to cost extra because it was kind of heavy but the guy did not charge us. Our flight did not leave until about 8:00 am. I was a nervous passenger because I don't care much for flying but I weathered through it.

We flew into Newark, New Jersey and arrived at about 10:30 am. I was very happy because I was getting very tired of carrying all that luggage. We finally made our way to the Rent-a-Car. . Now we were on our way to Brooklyn. It seemed like we had to go through ten thousand toll booths to get there but we finally made it.

I saw right off that the traffic was no joke in New York; the cab drivers are crazy. I don't see how they don't have more accidents than they do. But you know Laura knew how to handle the traffic. We went to see her father first while her mother was at work. It was a muggy day because they had so much rain come through.

Now you know Desiree had not asked about me none when she first went to New York for the summer. Now suddenly when I get to her grandparents' house, she was smiling in my face talking about did I miss her. I wanted to curse that little girl out but I played it off.

When we went to see Laura's aunt and cousin they greeted me so well. I felt good about the meeting. After that we went to check in at the hotel. It was nice but for $800 we should have had a refrigerator and microwave. Well later that evening we went back to her mother's house. It was time to meet Mama Minister. I must say it was not as bad as I thought it was going to be. Her mother was sitting on the couch feeding Laura's nephew. I thought her mother was very beautiful. She was very friendly towards me. It was a good meeting. We did not do much the rest of the evening. I think her mother was trying to hang with us if we were going anywhere to eat but we just went back to the hotel.

The next night was the get-together with friends and family. It was mostly family. We had a table of about 12. It was fun listening to them reminisce about the things that went on in their lives. I ended up sitting by her mom. I was still a little nervous but she made me feel comfortable. It also felt good that the friends who came knew about my relationship with Laura. Everyone accepted me. Now I was ready for some site seeing.

We went to Manhattan and walked down Time Square. I really enjoyed the night life. I took an album of pictures. After all it was my first official vacation. Laura's friends from the get together hung out with us every night. Then it was time to meet some more of Laura's friends. Since Laura and Desiree had an issue to work out, her mom said I was going to ride with her to a bar-b-que. Before we left, we had to wait for Laura's brother. He rode with Desiree and Laura. But back to her mom.

I had no idea what she was going to talk about because she said that she wanted me to ride with her so she could get to know me better. Laura had already told me not to be a punk so I did not disappoint her. I just spoke honestly about everything from my family to Cedric to Desiree to Laura. It seemed like it was going to be a long trip considering we had about a 45-minute ride but after we started talking it ended so quickly. Her mom also expressed some things about herself that I was surprised to hear her talk about. She made me feel very comfortable the whole ride there.

As for Laura's friends I enjoyed listening to how they would get into trouble and do all kinds of crazy things. It was nice seeing old friends grown up. During the get together, Desiree started getting upset because people were asking her about her father. But for the most part, that made her have an attitude with me. I think she was also upset at the fact that Laura's family welcomed me with open arms. I did not care to be around her while I was there but that was Laura's daughter.

After the bar-b-que, we went back to Laura's mom's house. Traffic was terrible. It took us twice as long to get back which really made for a long night. If I had known the drive was going to be that long, I would have driven for her mom. Once we did get to her mom's house, we dropped off Desiree. Now we were on our way to the hotel. Both of us were very tired so we just fell asleep.

The next day I got to hang out on 125th Street by myself. Laura was getting her hair braided and it took 8 hours. I ended up walking up and down the street checking out the stores and scenery. I got some nice CDs from the street vendor. It was so funny about the vendors. I guess they had to have a peddler's license to sell them. If the police came through, the vendors would just fold up the sheet they had their CD's laying on and walk away. Soon as the police left they were right back setting up the CD's.

I went to Marshall's and saw this guy get arrested for shoplifting. I also got a good deal on some Jordan sneakers. I also got to see the popular Apollo theatre. I did not take my camera with me because I did not want people to think I was a tourist. I think people knew I was anyway because when I would cross the street, I would wait on the sign to tell me when to walk. Most of the New Yorkers would just walk across. Not me, not after I saw how the cab drivers drive.

I knew that I could not stay on 125th Street for 8 hours so I ended up finding Magic Johnson's theaters. I watched Raiders of the Lost Ark just to waste time. I also knew I would get lost if I got off 125th Street. After the movie I went to check in with Laura. I guess I had been gone so long she said I made her nervous. She thought I was lost. But after that I just hung around the hair shop for the duration.

I was sitting on a porch next to the place. There was a club next door. I noticed a female in an SUV pull up and let someone out at the curb. I also noticed she had a gay sticker on her car. I asked her about places to go and she gave a few choices. Finally, Laura's hair was done. It was a long day so we just went to the hotel and tried to get rested up for church the next day. I was excited about dressing up for church. I wanted her people to see another side of me. Not the always "Tommy Hilfiger" clothes wearing tomboy.

I must admit Laura and I looked good for church. I was hoping my hair would survive the duration of the trip. Thank goodness it did. We were the first to arrive at church. Laura was making her rounds speaking to old friends. Then her parents, her aunt and her goddaughter came. The church service was nice. They did not have a choir that day and it was also dress-down day and I had on a skirt suit. During the service, it was time for people to go to the pulpit and pray. Laura, Desiree and Laura's friend went up. Laura's mom asked me if I wanted to go up and I said I was okay. Then she got my attention and said that I should never turn down a prayer. Next thing I knew, she took my hand and we went up to the podium. It was an experience I would never forget. She was telling me to forgive Cedric for what he did to my dogs.

After church, we took some more pictures and went back to Laura's mom's house. We changed clothes and went to eat for my birthday. I felt that I was very special. It was a buffet style restaurant. It was myself, Laura, her mom, her dad, Desiree and her nephew celebrating my birthday. At the end of dinner, they sung happy birthday to me. Again,

I was sitting next to her mom. I think she liked me or liked my spirit. She is an exceptional woman.

Later that night we went to one of the clubs the lady told me about. It was okay. There were not many people there. Two of Laura's friends went with us to celebrate my birthday. They all bought me a drink. I really enjoyed my birthday weekend in New York. We stayed out until about 1:00 am then we went back to the room. The next day was the walk around day. Laura put me on the train. It was so hot in the subway. We went to Madison Square Garden, the Empire State Building, Rockefeller Center, Ground Zero, and Radio City Music Hall. We walked a lot that day; my calves were sore for days.

After the day was over, we made our way to her mother's house to drop Desiree off. Afterward we went back to the hotel. The next day we just did our last-minute sights. We went back to 125th Street to take pictures. We were supposed to go out to a club but I was not feeling it. I just wanted to spend time with Laura. We were hardly ever in the $800 room except to sleep. When it was time to get ready to leave, we made sure everything was packed the night before.

Our flight left around 3:00 pm the next day. When we got up the next morning, Laura had some running around to do in downtown Brooklyn. Afterwards it was time to head to the car rental and return the car. We had good timing and arrived on time.

We got our boarding passes and we were headed to security. We had a couple of carry-on bags. One of the carry-on bags had to be checked because the machine detected an unknown object in the bag. We were pulled to the side while security went through it. I thought maybe it was the iron that the x-ray machine was picking up. While security was looking through it, Laura started laughing because that was the bag that had a surprise toy in it. I started laughing and then said so what. The security agent noticed it and looked at both of us and smiled.

Everything did check out and we were on our way to the terminal. We got a bite to eat before the flight. We had an hour before we could start boarding. Almost instantly we both fell asleep. We were kind of tired. We slept the entire trip back. Once we arrived in Atlanta, we grabbed a taxi and went to the condo. We did not pick "Max" up until the next day. Max was Cedric's dog who I was taking care of after he moved out. Yes, I was taking care of his dog. He had two but he left the other one dead in a dog house in the backyard. I believe he poisoned that one. Anyway, after the vacation things went back to normal. Laura and I talked about saving for our next vacation/cruise.

Labor Day rolled around and there was a party at Alison's house. We went and had a good time. Morgan was also there. We talked a lot and were subtle to one another. Laura, meanwhile was mingling her butt off. I think she had a good time. I don't think she cared for me talking to Morgan as much but I guess she understood. We met a lot of new people there. Sharon (my other best friend) did not make it. We did not stay long because we had to work the next day.

Later I had asked Laura if she wanted to have a fish fry toward the end of September. She said that would be cool. We pulled out my deep fryer I had not used since Monica bought it for my birthday two years prior. A few of Laura's co-workers came and everyone seemed to have had a good time. Everyone at the party knew about me and Laura so our relationship was no big deal.

A couple of weeks later, Laura's uncle came to Atlanta to visit his daughters and grandchildren. Laura went out to meet them for dinner. Right before he went back, she invited them to come over to her house for dinner. It was her, two cousins and their family. Desiree and I were not speaking again and I felt a lot of anger in the room from her while everyone was eating dinner. I caught her rolling her eyes at me a couple of times. One of Laura's cousins and her uncle felt the bad vibe from Desiree and asked her to chill. Desiree was supposed to spend the night but she got upset and her mother took her home to her dad's house.

After Laura dropped Desiree off, Desiree kept calling

the house. I guess she wanted to apologize like she usually does when she has figured out she was wrong but Laura had not made it back yet. Myself and one of her cousins talked about an hour and a half after she left. Through the conversations we found out that we had met before several years prior but under a different circumstance. I had actually met her while I was working at East Point Police Department. She was the lady in the overturned vehicle that I stopped to help. Now I was dating her cousin, Laura. What a small world. She had finally left about midnight but Laura was still not home yet. I started getting concerned about her because I knew she left around 10:30 pm and it is only about a 10-minute ride to her destination. I could not call her because she forgot her cell phone. After her cousin left, I started riding around the neighborhood trying to see if maybe she was in an accident or something. I could not find her. I decided I was going to go back by the house and then go look for her again. By the time I pulled up at the house she was calling me. I was so upset but glad to know she was alright. She asked me where I went and I told her I was out looking for her. She said she needed some time alone. I told her that was fine but the next time pull over and call me because I was worried.

After that everything went back to normal. I would spend most of my time at her house instead of my place since I did not have my dogs anymore. After a while she and Desiree started getting their relationship back in order. I was happy for that. Desiree and I still had our up and down days though.

One evening while Laura and I was watching TV, she said she had to tell me something but she was reluctant. I told her to just say it. She confessed to me that she had slept with Cedric on one of the occasions when she spent the night at his place. Did I want that to happen, no. But I think that ever since Laura admitted to sleeping with her husband while we were together, I began to withdraw from the relationship with her. At that point I just wanted her to get her relationship back with her daughter. I was very hurt by her sleeping with him but in the back of my mind I think I expected it because he was still her husband. Once things got good with her and her daughter, I was good.

Shortly after that conversation, Laura got word that her husband was losing his apartment and he had nowhere to go. Being the person that she is, she allowed him to come back and live with her so that her daughter could be with her. This was something I was not expecting but I told her if she wanted to do that then I would support her. She asked me to wait on her for two years until her daughter graduated from high school. She thought our relationship could withstand something like that. She had hoped Craig would have been moved out by then but that did not happen. Our relationship slowly died and we became just friends so again I eventually became single.

CHAPTER 15

Wrong is Wrong

One day while at work on patrol, I went inside a Day's Inn hotel lobby to take a break. There was a very beautiful lady behind the desk. I had seen her before but in passing in the area. She was cool to talk to. After a while I was eventually assigned to patrol only that area due to an increase in crime. Sometimes I would go there just to take a break and watch the news on Hurricane Katrina in the lobby. It started to become an everyday thing and it looked good to have a patrol car outside the business.

The lady's name was Bernice. Bernice was a heterosexual woman with three kids. She moved to Atlanta from Philadelphia about a year prior. I thought she was a very pretty woman. She was a plus size woman but things like that didn't bother me. We started having more conversations beyond work and we started getting to know one another. Weeks later, the more conversation we had, the more it became an attraction between the both of us. It had gotten to the point where I had started looking out for her kids at the bus stop because her oldest son had been jumped and robbed. Meanwhile, I was still friends with Laura and would still talk to her on occasions.

As I got to know Bernice, I also got to know her kids. Her daughter had a birthday coming up and I offered to buy the cake for her party. She was turning 5 years old and her dad came up from out of town. He was a real nice guy. He did not care about my sexuality; he just cared about the well-being of his daughter. When I first met her middle son, he was suspended from school. Her boys did not have their dads in their lives so she raised them by herself. Her oldest son was cool at the time.

As for me and Bernice, I think we started dating but did not even know we were dating. I remember we both went to a play by Tyler Perry. We were not sitting in the same area so we met in the lobby during intermission. That night she wanted to come back to my place. She spent the night and we were intimate. A couple of days later, she came over to my condo and we had a serious talk. She sat me down and told me about herself. She let me know she had been arrested but had become a changed woman. At first, I was saying not another Aubree. But again, I felt she had changed her life at least for her kids. I believed her because who was I to talk since I had been arrested also.

The next few months went well. Christmas came around and I tried to make sure everyone had a good Christmas. Bernice gave me a ring on our first Christmas. About three months later we ended up looking for a house to move into because I knew the condo was too small for all of us. I guess I moved fast because I wanted that family life but did not want to have my own children. She was also ready to move so that she could get her kids out of that area because they were getting in too much trouble. When her lease was up in April, they all moved into the condo temporarily. It was her, her daughter and her oldest son. We had taken her middle son to Alabama to live with a family member. By May, her daughter went to spend the summer with her dad and her oldest son was the only one still there.

Around July her middle son had returned. Things started going sour. I think her oldest son had gotten used to being the only kid in the house so he started having issues when his brother returned. I can remember her oldest son getting upset for no reason and started cutting up his brother's clothes. One day myself, Bernice and her middle son were in my room playing a game. Her oldest son acted like he did not want to be bothered with anyone so we left him in the other room by himself. After about 30 minutes we started hearing a bunch of noise in the room. I did not know he was literally tearing up the room and breaking furniture. I ended up calling the police on him. He was only 13 years old at the time but I did not care.

When the police officer arrived, he talked to him and asked him why he did what he did. He told the officer it was because his mother was dating a woman. An excuse he would use for the duration of Bernice and my relationship. The officer actually took his side. I ended up not pressing charges.

Shortly after this incident, we found a house. The house we moved into ended up being around the corner from the condo. I lied to my mother and told her I was buying the house but I knew I was not. We were renting. We rented it in Bernice name but I paid the bills. It was a three-bedroom, two bath home. We moved in and then things went from bad, to good, back to bad, back to good.

I had so many issues with her boys it was not even funny. Her daughter was such a sweet child. She was my daughter just as Alexis's youngest son was my son. I loved her to life. There was nothing I would not do for that little girl. She got good grades in school and she was a very respectful child.

It was April 30, 2007 and I was now a Marta Police officer. I must admit it was very different working for a transit police department. It put me closer to the dangers and elements of being an officer. Bernice and I were still together but the relationship was not where I wanted to be. Her sons were still very disrespectful until they needed something. I tried very hard to be a parent figure to them but it was just not working out. I was the bread winner in the household and I tried to take on that role. I had started feeling like I was being taken advantage of.

Bernice's oldest son started being very rebellious especially when I stopped helping him financially. He started getting into fights at school and started getting suspended. He was also starting to physically fight Bernice which would end up with me having the police come to my home. The part I did not like was the fact that I knew the officers who were coming because I had worked with that police department prior. When they were called, I would stay in my room while Bernice dealt with her son and the police.

As a police officer you can't have any type of domestic violence on your record. I thought it was best for me not to deal with that issue. I could possibly lose my certification and have to go through an internal investigation because of the domestic issue going on in my home. I can remember another incident with Bernice's oldest son. He got upset because we would not give him some money for something he wanted. I think he had more issues going on with him beside this one. Not to mention he was spoiled and he considered himself the head of the household because his dad was not around.

One night he attempted to commit suicide. After an argument with his mom, he cursed her out and then ran into his bedroom. I did not want to deal with it because I already had mental issues with a male disrespecting a woman. Bernice followed him to his room and I heard continued arguing between the two. Suddenly, I heard Bernice scream my name. I ran in the room and saw her fighting with her son because he had a knife in his hand and he was trying to cut his throat. I immediately intervened and we all struggled in the room trying to get the knife away from him.

When I finally got the knife from his grip, he then tried to leave the house but Bernice stopped him in the living room. I went and got my handcuffs and put them on him. Bernice decided to call the police. Again, my fellow officers responded to my house. We told them what happened and how he ended up in handcuffs. One of the officers was a female and the other a male. Her son was crying and saying he wanted to kill himself. The male officer tried to talk to him and asked him why he wanted to kill himself and he told the officer that he wanted to kill himself because his mom was dating a woman. Please…Really?

Everything was alright if he was getting the things he

wanted. Mind you, me and his mom had been together for three years already. He was looking for attention. So naturally by him saying he wanted to kill himself it was mandatory that he go to the hospital. Because he was a minor, the police and Bernice had to go with him. The police took the handcuffs off of him and took him to Grady hospital in the back seat of their patrol car. Myself and Bernice followed behind them. Naturally her son tells the doctor the same story which was a bunch of bull.

After the hospital visit, we had to take him home. Bernice tried to get the doctor to keep him a couple of days but they did not have a facility for a minor. After that episode, it was off and on with her son. He and his mom would still fight every now and then but I had really let go of the whole situation. There would be times where I would not even have a conversation with either son. The youngest son was following in the footsteps of his older brother. He too got into fights at school and ended up going to an alternative school. I would be the one to take him every morning to the bus stop to catch the bus. He was not as bad as the oldest. He was just very naïve and thought his brother was the coolest ever.

Now the next episode with Bernice's oldest son was the fact that he would steal from me. He would go into my closet and wear my clothes or even sell things that belonged to me. He sold clothing items, a cell phone and iPod. By this time, I really laid back from doing anything because I thought it would mess up my law enforcement career. At one point I got a key lock for my bedroom door so he could not just walk in my room and take things when I was not there. I even had to get a refrigerator and put in my room because he would eat and drink things that belonged to me. After I put the lock on my door, I still noticed my clothes missing. He was using a knife to get into my room. Again, I got a lock that would further prevent him from getting in. The second lock worked.

Things were settling down for a minute until another fight happened between Bernice and her oldest. This time she put him out. He came back and tried to get into the house through a bedroom screen. When he could not get in, he destroyed the mailbox. He also came back and started kicking the front door leaving dents in it. This was beginning to be too much. I was beginning to pull away from the relationship. I had already pulled myself away from the relationship with her two boys. As far as I was concerned, I only recognized her daughter and took care of her. The house was a house divided. I would have no conversation with her boys. I would go to work, come home and go straight to my room. I had even stopped cooking for them. I was really miserable. This became too much to bear and

I saw myself wanting out of the situation more and more but I knew Bernice would not be able to afford to live there by herself.

Now the end of 2008 I had started going through a lot of losses around November. On November 14, 2008 I lost an aunt. It was unexpected. This was the first loss of a few. A couple of days prior to Thanksgiving I was told that my grandmother, Elizabeth, was going to be placed in hospice. She had been sick for a few weeks and my dad told me she was not improving. In the back of my mind, I prayed she got better. I still hoped she would pull through.

Now on Thanksgiving Day I cooked for some friends. After dinner that night, we were getting ready to go out to a club. While I was getting dressed, I got a phone call from my mom. I thought she was calling to say happy Thanksgiving because she sounded pleasant on the phone. She told me my grandmother had passed away. I was so hurt. Bernice was there to comfort me and even her youngest son came and put his arm around me. Her boys were not affectionate people but that touched my heart.

Thanksgiving would never be the same. When I went to Mississippi for Grandma's home-going, it gave me and my cousins a chance to really bond. We made sure each of us had someone to turn to when needed. We were more than cousins. We were like siblings. I know my grandma would not want it any other way.

During this time, I was still trying to figure out how to get out of the situation/relationship because by now we were not sexually active. Bernice and I were more like roommates but I still loved her. Christmas rolled around again and everything was still the same. We did have a good holiday and that was only because of her daughter. She deserved a great Christmas.

After Christmas I started telling Bernice how I felt about our relationship. At first, I thought it would work better between us if we lived in a different household because I was getting exhausted watching her boys treat her like crap. I could not really do anything accept be a support for her because I did not want to lose my job over a domestic situation. She basically said she could not afford to live there by herself so I decided to hang in there.

On January 28, 2009 I got word that my grandfather was rushed to the hospital. He ended up being fine and was sent home the next day. Then on January 31 I went out to run some errands and I noticed I had a message on my cell phone from my mom. I decided to call her back and she sounded pleasant again but then she told me my grandfather had passed away. I had not driven out of my subdivision yet so I turned around and went back home. I just ran back in the house and straight to my room. I just dropped in a corner and cried. Bernice did not know what was going on and then I told her. It was so much for me to deal with. My relationship, the death of my aunt, the death of my grandmother and now the death of my grandfather. After I went back to work from my grandfathers homegoing, I decided to get another dog. I ended up getting two Chihuahua's. The breeder only had two left so I bought both of them. I just could not leave one behind. I named them Barron and Baby.

While back at work I had started befriending a co-worker named Megan. At first it was a cool working relationship. We would talk about some personal things sometimes a well. It started giving me another reason to enjoy leaving the house. After a while, the friendly conversations became flirtatious. Both of us were having issues with our mates and did not want to be in our current relationships. Eventually we got together romantically. This really made me want to leave my current situation more because she did not have a lot of drama following her. Now was it right for me to get involved with another woman while I was with Bernice? No, it was not but one thing led to another again.

After that, I would only talk to Megan while I was at work because I still lived with Bernice. I had already made up in my mind that I was going to move back into the condo. This decision was made prior to Megan and I intimate encounter. I thought it was best before I messed up my career with a domestic violence incident. The straw that broke the camel's back was one evening I chose to go to bed early because I really did not want to deal with her boys. I had turned my phone off for fear that Megan would call or leave a text message while I was at home. Bernice came in to ask me to use my phone. I did not think anything of it. Once she turned my phone on, she saw a text that Megan had left. It was romantic in nature. Then she called Megan and asked her how long we had been sleeping together. Megan did know about Bernice. She told Megan we had been together five years. I think Megan just hung up.

After she hung up the phone, Bernice went off on me. I kept telling Bernice to give me my phone but she would not. She just started arguing to the point where the kids started coming out of their rooms. I did not say anything. Bernice then started slapping me. She began fighting me and pushing me around the room but I did not fight back because I could have loss my job. I had started trying to get my things together to go back to the condo and just leave for good. She would not allow me to leave the bedroom. She kept pushing on me and cursing me out. At one point she grabbed me from behind and held me in a choke hold off my feet. I still did not fight back.

Bernice was much bigger than me. The fight moved into the bathroom and she pushed me in the tub. At that point, I had had enough. Once I got up, she began pushing and hitting me again. But I finally snapped and punched her in the face. I don't think it even affected her because she was so pissed off. I tried to walk out of the bathroom but she grabbed me again and began choking me more, picking me up off my feet. Her oldest son came in and tried to get her off of me.

By this time, I just wanted to get my uniform and go to the condo. At some point I attempted to call the police even though I did not want to because again I was afraid of having a domestic violence charge. When I tried to call, she pulled the phone out of the wall. I again tried to go grab some things and leave but I could not find my condo key. I really think she had it and would not give it to me. I tried to plead with her son to tell her to let me just get my things. I just wanted to leave with just my uniform so I could go to work the next day. Finally, she agreed to let me get my police uniform. I am sure she knew I was never coming back and it was over.

While I was getting my things, she threatened to contact my supervisors and tell them I fought her but she knew I was the one with the visible scars so she changed her mind. I was finally able to leave with both of my dogs (Barron and Baby) after that. When I left, I did not have anywhere to go. I just rode around crying. I ended up calling my good friend Laquata in the middle of the night and told her what happened. She was my co-worker. When we worked together people would not come around the station because we took almost everybody to jail. We worked well together. She told me to come and stay with her so I went to stay for the night.

Before I got to her house, I texted Megan to apologize to her. After I texted her, she started trying to call me but I was too afraid and embarrassed to answer. At some point I had finally answered and explained some things to her. We had agreed that we were friends first and before our sexual encounter.

Once I got to Laquata's house I went to the bathroom. This is where I saw how serious the marks on my neck were from Bernice choking me. I also noticed my right hand was swollen. I could not go to the doctor because I did not have the money for the co-pay. I did not get any sleep that night. I stayed up until 4:30 am and had to get ready for work at 5:30 am. Luckily, it was a Sunday and I was working at a transit station that was not so busy and it was away from everyone. I was glad about that because the marks on my neck were very visible. I think my right hand was possibly sprang very badly but it felt like it was close to being broken.

Later that day Bernice contacted me and had agreed to give me the condo key claiming she found it when I left. I went and got a few things to last me through the week. I also agreed to leave Baby with her because the kids wanted him and I took Barron with me. A few days after this incident I had to go to the gun range and do my yearly qualification with the police department. It was very hard considering I was right-handed but I did qualify because my job was my livelihood.

After I got some more of my things, Bernice made me give her pre-written checks for half of everything to help her pay for things since it was truly over and she knew I was going back to the condo. I wrote the checks for fear that she would try to make me lose my job just like Evelyn tried to do. A part of my conscience wrote those checks as well because I was the financial provider in the household. I basically paid her off and for the next three months I never had any money. I did not tell my mom I had moved back into the condo until 3 months later.

A week later I rented a U-Haul to get the rest of my things from the house. On moving day, I was catching hell trying to even pay for a U-Haul truck but I was able to figure it out. Bernice and I at least agreed on what furniture I was taking with me even though everything was mine and I paid for it all. The only problem was she would not let me go through my things. She basically had packed what she wanted me to take. She kept a lot of personal items like my laptop and a camera. My best friend Alison, her girlfriend and another friend of mine helped me move. I could not do much because my hand was still very painful and I could only carry things with my left hand. It was not hard to make that move but I did feel bad because I know I caused Bernice so much hurt but I knew it would not have lasted too much longer. I was truly unhappy in our relationship.

Once I moved back to the condo after my relationship with Bernice, I started working a lot. I was not home like I should have been with Barron so I gave him to a family member. In place of a dog, at one point I had geckos but they kept dying. I was still looking for something to come home to.

CHAPTER 16

Megan My Friend

Now I must admit I did not expect Megan to be by my side like she was after that ordeal. I am sure she sacrificed some things to make sure I had what I needed. She would also come over and make me meals for the week and make sure I had food to eat then she would go home and take care of her household. She constantly stayed by my side. She would spend a lot of time at my place just to comfort me. But at some point, I started to feel a little smothered. I had to let her know I liked her company but her family needed her home sometimes as well.

A few months later we had decided to have a get together at the condo. I can remember us having a wonderful time but when people started leaving we had a small disagreement. She was ready to call it a night but her cousin was still there. She went outside to have a smoke. She had a lot to drink so she was trying to sober up before she drove home. When I decided to go outside to sit with her, Megan approached me and kind of demanded I get in the house. Well, I did not feel as if I should have just left her cousin outside by herself. I stayed outside until her cousin got ready to go.

Now for Thanksgiving that year, I decided to go home and spend it with my family. All my cousins were home and we paid homage to my grandmother who had passed the year before. I really enjoy being around my family. Then it was time for Christmas. This was also the time in which I learned Megan was good friends with Ana, the woman who had been taking care of my Aunt Gladys and Uncle Johnny. Again, what a small world.

During the Christmas holidays, I was kind depressed because of my money situation due to Bernice. Megan's cousin had bought us tickets to go see Frankie Beverly and Maze. This was around January 1, 2010. After the concert I got upset with Megan because I thought she was going to go home because again she had been away from her kids a few days. I did not want constant company and I thought that was our understanding from the beginning.

When it came time for the Superbowl, we had a wonderful time. My good friend Cree and her girlfriend, my friend Donna, and her cousin came to watch the game at the condo. After this get together, Megan and I had started having a better understanding of each other. By April my cousin wanted me to come to her 40th birthday party and I went to Mississippi for about a week. After that, the next few months were good. Megan and I had set some more boundaries on the relationship. It helped that we were friends first.

A few months later, I decided to have some of Megan's friends meet us out to celebrate her birthday. We all met at Dugan's on Memorial drive in Atlanta. About 15 people came, including Ana, and we had a ball. The next few months Megan started spending more time at her house. I had also started taking online courses at St. Leo University. I was inspired to go back to school when I went to Cree's graduation. I only took one class the first semester until I got the hang of it. The next few semesters I took two classes each.

Thanksgiving came again. I decided to invite my parents up from Mississippi. My mom bought her famous dressing but I cooked everything else. The menu was candied yams, green beans, ham, turkey, mac and cheese, sweet potato pies, chitterlings, and potato salad. Megan's family came also. I also went to pick up my cousin Dee from Hillman. When it was time to eat, my dad had us all hold hands and he said the blessing around the table. That was a first for me because I could not remember us saying blessings before a meal. At least not that I can remember so that was very special to me. After the blessing it was on and popping. I really enjoyed this moment and this get together. I always enjoy when I can feel comfortable around my mom about my lifestyle.

For Christmas we decided to spend it at Megan's with her family since we did Thanksgiving at my condo. Everyone had a wonderful Christmas. It was the first time I felt like everyone was appreciating the things they received.

December 31, 2010 started like any other New Year's Eve. It was mandatory for me to work at Five Points Marta station. It was the location for the Georgia Peach drop. We had to shut down the station during the Peach drop. Unfortunately, after we started letting people back into the station, we had a youth get stabbed and killed by an adult. What a way to start off the New Year. Then a week later we had a person shot and killed in the same station. It was just a sad situation.

I have seen a lot while working at Marta Police Department. Because we were within the Atlanta city limits, we would also respond to calls in their jurisdiction. My area was known as The Underground. The Underground was a popular shopping area in Atlanta. I can remember responding to a call of a person shot behind it. When I arrived, I noticed a male lying on the ground with a gunshot wound. He was trying to breath. I was just trying to keep him alert until Atlanta Police Department and an ambulance arrived. I am not sure if he made it or not but when I left, he was still alive.

I have chased people through the Five Points Marta station for something as simple as not paying their fare. I actually escorted a male out of the station when I saw him walk in behind another patron. Later I noticed he decided to come back on the other side of the station and try to gain entry again. After I approached him this time, he jumped the gate and started running toward the platforms. I thought I had radioed for back up or at least let dispatch know where I was located in the station but I guess I was in a dead spot and they did not hear me asking for help. When I caught up with the male he had jumped on the train but the doors were still open. I guess the train operator saw that there was an incident on the train so he did not close the doors. I tried to get the man handcuffed but we ended up in a very physical altercation.

I was unable to contact my dispatch to request help, I just continued trying to subdue the man. During our fight I noticed patrons moving out of the way. At one point the man actually picked me up and body slammed me on the train. I did not realize he had body slammed me until I heard a patron on the train say, "He just body slammed that female police officer." All I could do was hold on to his leg until help arrived because he tried to exit the train. Finally, I saw other officers arrive and take him into custody. After I got up, I started hyperventilating from the adrenaline and my Sergeant was trying to calm me down. Yes, I had scrapes and bruises but I was fine. I was a tough cop.

I also remember an incident on a Sunday which are very slow days in the station. I noticed an intoxicated male walk in behind a patron without paying his fare. I radioed my dispatch to let them know I was out on a call. I approached him with the intention of telling him to leave because I did not feel like taking anyone to jail that day. He was a regular arrestee but I just wanted to have an easy day. He did not want to leave so again I radioed dispatch to let them know my location but again I guess I was in a dead spot in the station. He was ignoring me while he continued walking toward the platform. I approached him again but this time I attempted to handcuff him. I still did not have any backup officers respond yet.

Once I got within arm's reach, he punched me in the face. I don't know what happened but I became superwoman and had some power that came out of nowhere. I had so much anger at the fact that I was just punched in the face by a man. It took my thoughts back to my sexual assault when I was in the military. The next thing I knew, I had him face down on the ground by myself with one handcuff on and then another officer came to help me in detaining him. I really enjoyed taking control of him and the situation. I think that was the beginning of me realizing that I had an anger issue. He was ultimately convicted of assault on a police officer and sentenced to 5 years.

February 2011 came and I was really looking forward to getting the year off to a good start. I had started working extra because I wanted to save money. Megan and I had decided to just be friends. It worked out better and I thought it was best.

I saw a good year ahead of me even with my hidden anger issues. All I had to do was to stay positive and stay focused on my life goals. But on another note, I felt like the things that I have endured in my life was coming to a head. I was really having issues with men and had been since the rape but did not realize how it affected me until I became a person of authority like a police officer. I had also gotten to a point where my life was changing and I just wanted to be totally alone. Megan could see the change, but there was nothing she could do to help.

One day while at work I had a conversation with a co-worker. He got up the nerve to ask me if I gay. I smiled and said yes. It was a quiet night, so we just started talking. We were both prior military so we talked about that. At one point he asked me why I decided to date only women. I told him about the sexual assault in the military. I was comfortable talking to him because I could only trust the men who I worked with because they were my police family. I felt that as a fellow police officer they would protect me if needed versus harm me. This is when he told me I could apply for veteran benefits for P.T.S.D. He told me what to do and where to go.

I put in a claim with the veteran administration later that month. I then went through a psychological exam. I just hated the fact that they gave me a male psychologist to speak with. I did not think I had a choice of choosing a female psychologist. I had no idea I was possibly going through certain things because of the sexual assault. I had no idea that could contribute to my anger issues with men.

By March 2011 I had decided to seek some help. I started going to a psychologist. I, of course, chose a female. It's amazing how she was able to bring out so much that was hidden inside of me. I was holding so much of my life bottled up and I was still looking for love. Up until that time, I had been leaving one relationship and going directly into another one while hurting women along the way. In the beginning she said things may change with me and my relationships. She was right. The more I went to her, which was every week, the more I was taking a step back from needing to be in a relationship. I shared everything with her. I saw her for about the next six months.

Meanwhile after years of searching for my military roommate, I had finally found my friend Kathy on Facebook. I must admit I was very nervous when I contacted her because I still had a crush on her. She told me she was a Christian now and that she had given her life to Christ. I had no problem with that. I just wanted to reconnect with my friend—nothing more nothing less. We talked and caught up with one another's lives. I told her I would like to come visit her. She said that was cool and that I could stay at her house if I liked.

Now back to my therapy sessions. I began to see a change in me. At one point I did not want to deal with being in a relationship with women. I just wanted to be alone. But I quickly found out being alone for me meant a state of depression. I did not feel suicidal but I was feeling depressed because I knew my life was not supposed to be this way. At one-point my therapist prescribed me a drug called Cymbalta. It was an anti-depressant. I took it for about 3 months. I had also spoken to my therapist about my dogs being killed. I told her they were the one thing that I knew would love me unconditionally. I used to look forward to coming home to my dogs even when there was not a human to come home to. My therapist suggested I look into getting another pet.

Now that I was in a place where I was doing better financially and did not work extra jobs, I went on the internet to look for another Poodle. Low and behold I found a brown poodle at the Humane Society in Fayetteville, Georgia. The next day I went and picked up what would be my Chico. He was found roaming a neighborhood and had been in the Humane society for about a month. His hair was long and matted but I knew he was the pet for me. I considered him my therapy dog. Chico really brightened my day. It was me and Chico against the world. I was back happy and looking forward to getting home to Chico every day. Before him I would just sit in my living room with candles lit, listening to very sad music and drinking Corona until I got sleepy. Megan and I were not speaking as much. I kind of went into a me, myself and I mode but I still continued my therapy sessions because they were helping.

CHAPTER 17

My Future

Now it was getting close to the time for me to visit Kathy. A couple of times she was having second thoughts because she knew I had expressed how I felt about her. She did not want to visit any uncertain feelings because she had converted to Christianity and it would be wrong for her to express those feelings. I convinced her that I am only coming to visit a friend. I told her that I respect her and her Christian belief. I just wanted to visit a long-lost friend.

She finally agreed to allow me to visit. I must admit I was nervous when that day came. I bought some new clothes for the trip. During this time, Kathy was in school completing a master's degree. She was working and going to classes. When it was time for me to head to the airport, I was very excited. Once I landed, the butterflies kicked in. I did not know what to expect. I had on some K-Swiss sneakers, khaki shorts, white t-shirt and an orange plaid shirt. I was being myself. I got my luggage and waited for her on the curb.

When I first saw her, it was like looking at my old military roommate. I also saw the woman I still had a crush on. I am not sure how she felt but I was happy to see her. When we got in the car, I think both of us were nervous. We went to get something to eat and then went to her beautiful home. I thought it was rather large for just one person but it was a beautiful home. I unpacked my clothes and we just chilled the rest of the day. I can remember us sitting in her family room watching T.V. I think Kathy was tired because she had fallen asleep in the chair and I did not bother her. The rest of my stay we ate out mostly because Kathy did not cook much but I did not mind. She also took me site seeing. I think every night we stayed up late just talking. My stay seemed so short but I had to go back to work.

In my mind from my first visit, I had made Kathy my girlfriend. I visited every month after my August visit. I think it was my September visit when she asked me to think about moving to Maryland. She said there were great opportunities in the DC area and she would take care of me. I went back home and I thought about it. I knew I was entering year 20 as a police officer and I thought maybe it was time for a new career. I loved my job very much but I also loved Kathy. I was willing to pack up my life for her. I had never had anyone say that they would take care of me. I had always been the one taking care of other people.

When I got back from my September visit, I started looking for jobs in that area because I did not want to leave Georgia without having a job in place. Being a police officer was the last thing I really wanted to do. I knew I would have to go through the police academy again but being a police officer was all I knew. I did have a few police departments that invited me to take a test. I remember taking one for Arlington Sheriff Department. I did not mind working back in a jail versus on the streets. I received a letter from the department saying that I had passed the test. I thought this was going to be the job I got because I had more than enough experience. They sent me other paperwork to fill out in order to go to the next step. (Now remember I had been arrested over 13 years ago). I thought I was doing the right thing by letting them know. Shortly after I divulged that information, I was no longer a candidate for the department. I was very hurt because I was had been able to be a police officer after the arrest.

Well, I came to visit Kathy in October for a quick trip. The next month was her birthday month and she was turning 50. I made plans to come and stay about 10 days. By now I had already made up my mind to make a move to

Maryland. This is the time where I wrote my mom a long letter explaining my military sexual assault and my moving to Maryland. In my mind, all I heard from my mom was if I really wanted to move to Maryland. She really did not speak on the sexual assault. That was how I communicated mostly with her, through writing letters.

Well it was now time for my November visit. I took Chico to be boarded and I headed out to celebrate Kathy's 50th birthday. I stayed at her home with her cousin and three other childhood friends. Kathy had pretty much had everything in place for the party. While I was there for this visit, I hung out with her family and friends. I slept in the basement but at night Kathy would sneak down there and either fall asleep with me or get a goodnight kiss. On one of these days, we all went to B. Smith's restaurant at Union Station in Washington DC. Afterwards we walked around and looked at the stores. Kathy saw some boots she wanted and I got them for her. I felt all eyes on us by her friends but I did not care. I am sure they were wondering what was going on. Even at the dinner table they kept asking Kathy about her so-called date that she went on several nights before I got there. I think she told them that to keep them off our tracks. As for the party, I think everybody had a great time.

Thanksgiving was coming up but it was time for me

to go back. I did not mind because I was going to be moving there in a couple of weeks. I got back and prepared myself for my move to Maryland. I even sold my motorcycle. It was hard to turn in my two-week notice. It was also very hard to leave my friends and my comfort zone of 30 years. I believe I gave up a lot to be with the woman I thought was going to be with me for the rest of my life. I did not have a job but I had money to last me several months. Besides, Kathy said she was going to take care of me. I packed up my car with what I could take and I packed up Chico and took him out of his element. Kathy had never had dogs before so it was a first for her. I was willing to leave Chico with Alison until she was comfortable enough to allow him into her home. It was about a ten hour drive but we made it safely.

In January 2012, I received a letter from veterans' administration saying they were approving my military benefits for my P.T.S.D. I was also given benefits for Temporomandibular Joint Disorder (TMJ). That at least gave me some type of monthly income while I was unemployed.

Our first few months went well. One day we went to Costco and as soon as a walked in the store I saw something that made my heart start beating faster and my anger boiling up in my head. I ran across Cedric. The same man who killed my dogs. We made eye contact. He evidently worked there because he was pulling a cart. I just could not believe I was seeing this man. I knew he had family in Maryland but I never thought I would ever see him again after he killed my dogs. I quickly told Kathy and we left.

The months that followed were difficult. I started having doubts about my move. I knew I may have made a move that should have waited. After all, we did not really know each other. I allowed a crush and lust to move me into an unknown area. Kathy did not get to know me and I did not get to know her. That was not a good combination. I guess I was thinking I was moving in with the same woman from 1986.

I had certain ways she did not like and she had ways I did not like. After the first 90 days I really wanted to go back home but then again I wanted to make the relationship and career change work. I had left my job, my home and my friends to move to a place where I did not know anyone nor did I have a job. I thought we could work things out and just talk through everything.

The next few months Kathy and I had good days and bad days. By June 2012, I finally got a job with a security company. I was back in uniform working 12-hour shifts. I was assigned to the Department of Justice (DOJ) where the Attorney General Eric Holder's office was located. It was an okay job but I really did not want to work 12-hour shifts and stand in the elements, hot or cold.

I had also transferred to the University of Maryland University College (UMUC). I started my classes in August. While at work I met this woman who seemed to be cool. I did not know she was gay at first. She was cool to have conversations with. At the same time, during our relationship, Kathy and I were having a lot of disagreements. So a decent conversation was always welcomed. I did not like drama and I did not do drama.

I must admit the woman was cute and there was an attraction between us but I did not take it beyond conversations. We exchanged numbers and would text every now and then. I don't know how Kathy found out about her but she did and all holy hell broke loose. Once Kathy felt that we were seeing each other I had to convince her I was not seeing or having relations with her. This lasted until New Year's 2013. Kathy wanted me to text her and I did. All I said was Happy New year and she texted back the same. I guess Kathy was waiting to see something more but there was no more to see.

I must admit our relationship was never going to be the same after my emotional affair. Kathy would never trust me again. This was one of the times where we thought about separating but I never left. If I did leave, I would leave long enough for both of us to cool down. That was how the next few months went.

Now her mom lived about 10 minutes away. In the beginning her mom was fond of me but when she found out I was dating her daughter everything changed. Her mom was not really speaking to me. I did not understand why.

By then I really started feeling like I should have stayed in Atlanta. I was in a place where I was having disagreements with my girlfriend and I felt like her mom did not like me. Not to mention I did not have any friends in Maryland. The next few months we continued to have disagreement. At least that's how I felt about things between Kathy and I. Kathy was the type that wanted to talk about things then and I was always the one who would shut down and not want to talk. Sometimes I felt that when I did express myself or apologize to her she did not want to hear it or it made her more upset. I just did not know how to communicate.

What I actually found out was that Kathy and I were very different. We did not do much of the same things. Kathy was the type who would do things right then and there and I would get to it when I would get to it. I have to admit I am a procrastinator. The only time I would follow-up with doing things was after a disagreement but when the air cleared I would get back to my old self. A lot of times I tried to see if I was a bad mate for Kathy. Sometimes I saw where I was wrong and I would apologize. There were also times where I did not think I was wrong but I would still apologize. I just wanted to keep the peace.

Our holidays were okay but it seemed like something always came up and there would be a disagreement but we always got through our rough patches.

Christmas 2013, Kathy's mom gave me a gift. This was not your ordinary materialistic gift. She actually wrote me a letter. This was not an angry letter. This was a letter of apology for how she had been treating me. She was very sincere because it made her cry as she read it to me. I had to try and put myself in her shoes and understand how she felt about Kathy and our relationship. I am sure it was very hard for her to accept and it was new to her as well as Kathy. I accepted her apology and we have been good ever since. She has turned into a second mom for me.

The year 2014 was full of classes for the both of us. We were both set to graduate the following year. For me it was a normal year just like the others. This was also the year I started having medical issues. By May, I had to have surgery to remove some fibroids. This was the first time my parents came to Maryland since my move. I did not know Kathy had asked them to come because I had never had to have surgery before. Kathy was always trying to make me happy and she knew how much my family meant to me.

While at the hospital, one thing I never experienced was a catheter. I had no idea that little tube was supposed to go somewhere I had never imagined. So I started Googling everything from the procedure to how the catheter was going to be place in me. I will never forget the pain of it going in but it felt really good when the nurse pulled it out. If it was not for the tube coming from under the sheet, I would not have known I had something in me to catch my urine.

I can remember asking Kathy if I was supposed to urinate in the tube and she said, "You already did." We both just laughed. When they took me down for surgery, Kathy went as far as she could. After surgery, Kathy said she found me in the hallway unattended. I guess the orderly who was supposed to pick me up forgot me. She was extremely upset about that incident.

Once I got to the room I was told I had to lay flat so that I did not break a stitch. But what they did not do was have some pain medicine on board when I got back to my room. Again, Kathy was upset and made them bring me some morphine. After that morphine kicked in I was a happy camper. I ended up staying in the VA hospital for three days. My parents stayed a few days afterwards and my mom made sure we had food for a couple of days before they left to go home.

October 2014, I got offered a position as a security assistant with the federal government. That is what I wanted prior to my anticipated college graduation date. Kathy had been taking care of me financially while I finished school. I had not worked for at least a year. The position did not pay much but it was a promising career choice. The following year Kathy and I were both set to graduate May 2015. It was hard for me to get through my last semester because I had to pass statistics. If it was not for my classmates, my cousin and my co-worker's niece, I may not have made it. My ultimate goal was to graduate before I turned 50 and for my parents to see me graduate college and walk across that stage.

Now back to my new job. My co-workers were very nice. They allowed me to work on school papers during down time. They were a big help. Now the job required that I go to training out of state. February 2015, my boss had scheduled me for a week-long training in Boston. Around the same time as my class, DC was getting a lot of snow. I did not think it would affect my class but it did.

Sunday was my day to travel and I was all packed and ready for my flight the next morning. I received confirmation that the class was still going on prior to me leaving. Monday morning, I headed to the airport to fly to Boston before the snow got worse. Once I landed and check my phone for messages. I had a message from the class coordinator saying that the course was canceled due to the snow. I was in panic mode because the snow was getting worse to the point that they were starting to cancel a lot of flights out. I scrambled to call my supervisor to ask him what I need to do to get back home. He told me to contact the travel representative and see if they could find me a flight back to DC.

As soon as I contacted the representative they said that all flights to DC were canceled. I was almost in tears. I didn't want to be stuck in Boston. I called my supervisor to update him and he suggested I contact the travel representative again to see if I could get an Amtrak ticket to go back to DC. The representative was able to find a ticket for Amtrak but I would have to pay for it. Fortunately, I had enough money in my account for the one-way ticket. The only problem was I had less than an hour to get from the airport to the Amtrak station so I grabbed a cab hoping that I had enough time to get there through the snow. Once I got in the cab the driver told me it was about a 20-minute ride. I was in tears and praying that I make it. I had to get there and then purchase my ticket. Thank goodness I did make it and I was able to buy my ticket with the last of the money in my account. After my train left Boston they started canceling the remainder of the trains out of the station.

I had not ridden a train as an adult in a while. I got on the train and settled in for a six-hour ride. For most of the way I had a seat by myself. When we started getting in Pennsylvania it started to get crowded but I did not care. My only concern was that I was on my way back home. My train did not arrive until late at night. I know Kathy does not like driving in the dark so I think she was a little frustrated because she got lost trying to find the station. Now back to work and school.

In April 2015, I remember being told that my grandmother, Corene, was being placed in hospice. I did not realize she was sick. I remember visiting her in the nursing home a few months earlier. I knew she had dementia but she always knew who I was. One day while on my way to work on the Metro, I got a call from Kathy. She told me my grandmother had passed. I just instantly started crying in the middle of the station. I went home and Kathy started looking for us a plane ticket to go to Mississippi. When it was time to go to the airport, we were running late. When we got to check in, we were so late that they had given one of our seats to a person on standby. Kathy told me to go ahead and I began running to the gate. Kathy quickly caught up with me. Kathy would have to catch the next flight that evening. I told her not to worry about it that I would be fine. I now regret that I did not allow her to come with me and support me. I did not understand how much that hurt her. At the time I was only thinking about me getting there and not thinking about how Kathy wanted to be there also. I was being very selfish. It was also very devastating to know that my grandma was gone and it was two weeks before Mother's Day. It made it really hard to deal with. I had already bought her a Mother's Day card.

After that, it was hard to concentrate on my upcoming graduation in May. When Mother's Day did come around, I celebrated with Kathy, her mom, her aunt and her cousins. Kathy bought everyone tickets for a Mother's Day dinner cruise. It was hard for me since I had just lost my grandmother and the fact that I was not with my own mother who just lost her mother. It was sad but I was glad I was surround by Kathy's family and they showed me nothing but love.

The following week I was scheduled to go to class in Boca Raton, Florida. This was the same class that was scheduled for Boston but it was offered in Florida. This class was a week-long. This class was the same week as Kathy's graduation. I had already made up my mind that I was going to try to make her graduation on that Friday. Normally classes end early on Friday so I had changed my flight to an earlier flight. I left around 1:00 pm but my flight was not going to arrive until 3:00 pm. Kathy's graduation was set for 4:00 pm. I would have to get off the plane, get my luggage, take a cab to the rent a car location and then drive in traffic to Howard University.

Needless to say, I did make it just in time to her graduation. When I got there, I saw her mom and then I saw Kathy. I walked up behind Kathy and the look on her face was priceless. It made me feel good that I could be there for her. She just did not know I spent my last on changing that airline ticket but it was worth it. The following week it was time for my graduation. My parents, and Kathy's cousin came to support me. Kathy also surprised me with my best friend Alison.

That Friday night Kathy spent the night with her mom. The next day was graduation. My parents and Alison rode together and Kathy, her mom and her cousin rode in another car. I drove separately because I had to be there early. When my University of Maryland University College class of 2015 lined up and walked into the arena, I could see my parents and Alison on one side and Kathy, her mom and her cousin on the other side. They may not have been sitting together but I was glad all of them were there to support me.

After graduation, Kathy had a get together for me at Andrews Air Force base for all our friends. My mom's childhood friends even came to help celebrate. I think everyone had a good time. The next day everyone went back home. Now I am really getting into my job and learning a lot. Kathy and I were getting a little better. This was the time that I would have to give up my silver bullet (Pontiac Grand Prix). Most of the cars I had my dad played a big part in helping me pick them out. When I got rid of my (silver bullet) I told him I was looking at some Kia vehicles. Kathy had an extra vehicle she let me use while I looked for a new car. By August, my dad sent me a picture of a Kia Optima but it was in Mississippi. He told me it was fully loaded. I think my dad enjoyed helping me in any way that he could. He was always looking out for me.

I completed the paperwork, bought the vehicle and my dad picked it up. Later I had made plans to go to Mississippi to pick it up. I flew down on a Thursday. Kathy wanted to help me drive it back to DC since it was a 14-hour drive so she flew into Atlanta. I left Mississippi on Saturday morning and had to pick Kathy up at the Atlanta airport that same evening. We stayed at the condo overnight and got up early to drive back to DC. We made a stop in North Carolina to visit Kathy's aunt and cousin. That also gave us time to rest a little from the drive. We hung out a few hours and then got back on the road. I was very excited with life. I had a government job, I graduated college before turning 50, I had a new car and Kathy and I had been doing better.

That following year, 2016, Kathy had planned my 50th birthday party at Ft. Myers Club. Again, my parents and her cousin came. My aunt Sandie was also there. Kathy also invited a few of the Chicago and Baltimore steppers to the party. Her family also came to help me celebrate.

I could not do some of the things financially that Kathy had done for me since living with her. I really appreciated everything she did and still does. Kathy has been such a support for me and my family. She has a great heart and I believe there is nothing she would not do for me or my parents. Our relationship may have started off rocky for most of our first years together but for some reason we never left each other. I must admit that I had never been in a relationship like that. Meaning that I have never had to realize the issues I had within myself. I have always had an issue communicating when it was most important. I was so use to just walking away from a situation without talking about the issue at hand. We are now in a better place. We still have our moments of disagreements but we are communicating better to resolve them. I think both of us have some issues that we need to resolve within ourselves. I feel that is why we had so many disagreements. But as time went on we were able to acknowledge those things and work on ourselves and our relationship in a better way.

The following year, 2017, I started having medical issues with my breast. I always got my mammogram every year but this year was different. After my appointment I had to wait to speak with the radiologist. She told me that she saw some calcifications in my right breast and suggested an ultrasound breast biopsy. I was extremely nervous but Kathy was there for me like she has always been. After this procedure I had to wait for the tissue sample to be tested. When I got the call from my radiologist, she said that she suggests that I have surgery to remove a larger sample. I was scheduled to have a second biopsy. I actually had to go into a surgery room for this procedure. During this time, I had a favorite song and when I went into the surgery room my song was playing so I felt very comfortable. The song was, "Bruno Mars, That's What I like". I heard the first verse and then the anesthesia kicked in.

This time after this procedure it left my breast bruised to the point it was purple and green but that was a sign that it was healing. After that result came back it was benign. I was very happy to hear that. But because of that I had to start getting a mammogram every six months.

Toward the end of the year, we decided to move from Maryland because we were having so many problems with our basement flooding. While I was living there, the basement had flooded twice. So around September, we started getting the house ready for sale. By October, we put it on the market. By the end of October there was a contract on the house. We were not ready for the house to sale so quickly so we had to rush and find somewhere to live.

We ultimately chose to live on Joint Base Anacostia Air Force Base. By mid-November 2017, we were spending our first Thanksgiving and Kathy's birthday on the base. We thought we were going to be on base for 6 months but living on base was so convenient to our jobs. We also had a beautiful view of the Potomac River and Ronald Reagan Airport. We had actually gotten spoiled by not having to drive that long distance anymore and we found out that the base had a shuttle to drop us off in front of our work-place. We decided to stay until we were ready to make a move to the Virginia area.

December, I started having more medical issues with the joints in my hands, knees, elbows and ankles. I couldn't even tolerate Kathy trying to rub on my hands because it hurt so bad. I finally made an appointment and they decided to do some bloodwork. When the results came back, they referred me to a rheumatologist because something was abnormal about my test results. At my appointment, they did a physical exam and then left the room to read over my test results. The doctor came back in the room and told me I had Systemic Lupus Erythematosus (SLE).

Systemic lupus erythematosus (SLE), is the most common type of lupus. SLE is an autoimmune disease in which the immune system attacks its own tissues.

This diagnosis did not register with me at first because I felt unphased. The doctor prescribed some medication for me to take. When I did get in the car, I called Kathy and told her I have Lupus and again I was unphased but Kathy got quiet for a few seconds. It was not until I got home that it hit me. I started crying and telling Kathy I did not want to die.

I did not know much about Lupus. I thought it was a type of cancer. I had my moments of depression with the thought of my immune system being compromised. After a few months I started getting used to the lupus but now it was time for my six-month mammogram appointment again. After these results, the radiologist saw something again and she wanted to schedule me for an MRI breast biopsy. So, as well as being told I have Lupus (February 2018) I again had to deal with the issue of my breast again. The MRI breast biopsy was something that I would never want to go through again. It took about 2 hours. I was face down in a MRI machine and they were sticking a needle in my breast to get more samples. Fortunately, the results came back negative again.

The next few months I was still getting used to this

thing called Lupus. I was constantly searching the web for Lupus information. This is where I found a Lupus walk in DC. I must admit that before being diagnosed, I would have never thought about participating. I got further information and reached out to my friends and family for donations to find a cure.

Prior to the walk, they had a mix and mingle party. It is here that I met my Lupus sister. Victoria and I have been friends ever since. When it was time for the walk my dad came up to walk with me which was very special. (I will always be daddy's little girl.) This particular weekend was also Mother's Day so Kathy had plans with her mom to go out of town but she did the walk with me and my dad before she left. After the walk, my dad and I picked up a few philly cheesesteak sandwiches and relaxed the rest of the weekend.

The summer of 2018 I started having issues at my job. I was getting burned out and wanted to find another job. I wanted to enter a different career field, Personnel Security. I spent plenty of time applying for jobs with USA jobs. While I was applying for jobs, I took the initiative to complete several courses of training in that career field. Now when I did get chosen for interviews, the outcome was always the same. I had the courses but I did not have the experience. It had gotten so depressing for me. I was irritated at work and I really was not myself. I would do just enough at work and not anything extra and that was not me.

Around October 2018, my coworker got a new position and I was very upset. I did not feel she deserved to be the first to get another position. I felt upper management was playing favorites. I felt like I was the better employee and I was being taken advantage of in the office.

Thanksgiving 2018 rolled around and I cooked for Kathy and her mom. When Christmas rolled around, Kathy had asked my parents to come and spend the holidays with us. This was one of her many surprises because I did not have any family here with me. Kathy was always trying to make me happy and make sure that if I missed my family, she would send me to see them or she would bring them to me.

Around February 2019, it was my one-year anniversary for my Lupus diagnosis. I was also still concentrating on finding another job. In March I got an interview for a Personnel Security Specialist with the Small Business Administration which is the career field that I was looking for. I actually thought I did very well in the interview. Several months had gone by so I just thought they chose someone else so back to the drawing board. By now I really hated going to work but I knew I had no choice. Kathy was very supportive and she pushed me in a professional way and just told me to stop complaining and do something about it. I continued applying for other jobs. I would at least apply for two jobs a day. I did not want to give up on finding that position in the career field that I wanted but it was hard. I took leave when I could because I did not want to be in the office but I always stayed professional with the customers.

By September, I had received an interview with the Secret Service as a Security Specialist. If I got chosen for the position I was going to take it just to leave my current position. Again, I thought the interview went well. After the interview, the supervisor for the position asked me for my supervisor contact information. None of my other interviews went like that. They never asked for my supervisor contact information. I felt like I was going to be offered the position. By the end of the week, my supervisor came in and said he received a call from the Secret Service. He said, "So I guess you are going to be leaving soon." I was so happy. I knew I had the job.

By the following week on Monday, I got a call from Human Resources for the Secret Service. They officially offered me the position and of course I said yes. It was also a promotion from my current grade. It may not have been my Personnel Security Specialist position that I wanted but it was still a good job offer and my way out.

While driving home on that Wednesday I receive a call from Small Business Administration asking me if I was still interested in a Personnel Security Specialist position. This was from the interview I had back in March. I thought they had chosen someone else. Before I could catch myself, I told them yes also. Now I had two jobs that I had accepted. I went home and weighed out the pros and cons. The Secret Service required working shift and weekends. The Small Business Administration position schedule was Monday – Friday and telework from home. I think we all know which one I picked. Can you say happy? I was finally leaving the Office of Personnel Management. The Small Business Administration decided to take a chance on me even though I did not have the experience. I was definitely going to prove to them and myself that I would be the perfect fit for their organization. I had two weeks left at my current job. On my last day it was a little sad because I had a good repour with a lot of people in my building because I had been there for 5 years and I worked in customer service. My team was not bad, it was just really time for me to move on. To this day, I still keep in touch with a few of them. I also met a lot of Lupus friends at the building that I keep in contact with also.

Now it was time for me to go to my orientation for

my new position. The first day was an all-day orientation. During our lunch, one of my coworkers came and took me to our office. When I walked into our suite, I saw my name on an office door. First off, I had no idea I was getting my own office. I had a window, two desks and two computer monitors. I had really moved on up. I had a new work home. Once everything settled, I got to know my new team and everyone was very welcoming. I worked from home two days a week and the base shuttle dropped me off a few blocks from my job. I no longer had to drive into work.

The next Thanksgiving went very well. Kathy had finally traveled to Mississippi with me. She only stayed the weekend but I was glad she went. I drove her around to see my family and my birthplace. She enjoyed seeing my family history. Christmas went well also. I was able to get Kathy some of the things she actually needed and wanted for Christmas. Previous Christmas's had not been that great but I think I made up this year for the failed Christmas's. For New Year's we spent it at home watching TV.

Now it's 2020 and Kathy and I are doing great. Now March rolled around and there was something in the world that would change everyone's lifestyle and health. China had talked about the spread of the Corona virus (COVID-19). This meant a lot of people were beginning to get sick and also dying. The President called it a Pandemic. The world began to struggle and the virus began to spread. The grocery stores were out of stock on many things such as toilet paper and hand sanitizer. Many states put a "stay home" order out for people for two weeks. All restaurants, gyms, movie theaters and many other businesses were ordered to close. Only business that were deemed essential were to stay open like the grocery stores and gas stations. Thousands of people died and they predict many more would succumb to the virus. Not only was I thinking about how to stay healthy but because of my Lupus I was at a high risk to contracting the virus because of my weakening immune system. I had to be careful not to be around people. Everyone was to stay at least 6ft from each other and wear a mask. Wearing the mask would soon be the new normal.

CHAPTER 18

My Hero is Gone

My dad was a very gentle man. He was my hero, my protector, my friend, my father, my daddy and my poppy. He was very active in his church and he was always there for his family. I thought my dad was superman. In my eyes there was nothing he could not do. To me my dad was invincible but I found out that even the strongest of men have challenges.

March 2020, right before COVID, my dad started having issues with his legs. He was complaining about his legs being weak. He had test done but while we were waiting on the results, he fell at home and had to be taken to the emergency room. They conducted more test and then sent him home. While waiting for all the results, he started complaining about chest pains. He was taken to the emergency room again but this time he was admitted. When all the test results came back, it showed that he had multiple myeloma. (Multiple Myeloma is a blood cancer). After more test were done while he was admitted, they found that a nerve was pressing up against his spine which caused the weakness in his legs. Further test found that he had multiple myeloma on his ribs. Basically, he was not able to walk because of the multiple myeloma and the nerve that was pressing on his spine.

My dad had to have spinal surgery. It was really affecting me. I could not be there with him because they were only allowing one person in the hospital with the patient because of the Corona virus. Thankfully my dad's surgery was successful. I was just grateful that my mom was able to be with him during this time. My dad was still not able to walk so he was going to be given infusion shots for the cancer and go through rehabilitation for his legs. It was a long road ahead for him because he had to heal from the spinal surgery first in order to handle rehab. He stayed in the hospital for about a month. I had faith in God that my dad would walk again and get back to his normal self.

A week after he was released from the hospital, I took the 14-hour drive to be with him. I was very fortunate to have a supervisor that would approve me to work from my parents' home during this time. I must admit I was afraid of seeing my dad because I did not know what to expect. I was not used to seeing him dependent on anyone else to do things for him. He was always the one helping others but now he needed help. Based on my parent's relationship I wanted to make sure my mom did not get frustrated with being his primary caregiver. I had a conversation with my parents about working together through this ordeal and it went well. My mom was taking very good care of my dad. The next week he started his home rehab and he was progressing very well. The first few months he was going to his weekly appointments for his infusions. Twice a week he was transported in an ambulance on a stretcher. I had a talk with my mom about changing the way he was transported because I did not like seeing him be put on a stretcher. I convinced my mom to have my dad transported in a medical van in his wheelchair. I can't begin to imagine how he felt not being able to be himself but I told him that we will get through this but he had to be patient.

The months that followed my dads' release from the hospital, I made it a point to be with him almost every other month to try and help my mom out. It was also great to see the progress my dad was making during his at home rehab. I would try my best to keep him encouraged and positive. In 2020 I also made it a point to be there for Fathers' Day, Thanksgiving and Christmas. It hurt my heart every time I would have to leave him because I would always see him looking out the front door from his chair as

I drove away.

I don't know how he felt knowing that he had cancer and sometimes I would see him in deep thought so I would always try to beat him at dominoes or checkers to get his mind off of his illness. He loved playing those two games and he always loved to win.

By April 2021, I saw my dad stand and walk across the room on a walker. I was so elated. He was also able to get in and out of the bed by himself into his wheelchair. I knew my dad was really trying hard to walk again. My next visit was scheduled for Fathers' Day. In May, I noticed something had changed. He was not the same when I would talk to him on the phone. In mid-May, my mom had to call an ambulance for my dad because he was not eating and his breathing was not good. When they arrived at the hospital they discovered that my dad had pneumonia. The doctors had to remove fluid from his lungs to help him breath better. He was in the hospital for about a week and it seemed like he was bouncing back. I had spoken to him while he was in the hospital and my mom even sent me a picture of him eating. After that week they sent my dad home. The next few days he began not feeling well again. He was again admitted for the pneumonia and again they had to remove more fluid from his lungs. This time while he was in the hospital they found a lump on his neck which prompted the doctor to run more test. They allowed him to go home a few days later. The next few days at home my dad had stopped eating totally and he was not able to have a conversation. A couple of days later the doctor called my mom with the results of the lump. My dad was now diagnosed with Non-Hodgkin Lymphoma. My dad had two different types of cancer in his body. The doctor wanted to schedule a full body scan to see how they would treat both. I can clearly remember that the PET Scan was scheduled for Monday, June 7, 2021 and they had a follow-up appointment for the results on Wednesday, June 9, 2021. For me, those were the longest two days in my life. When Wednesday came around all I could do was wait for my mom to call me. The phone call finally came and my mom told me that the non-Hodgkin had taken over my dad's body. She then told me that my dad was going to be placed in home hospice. I just dropped to my knees and started crying.

I called Kathy because she was at her moms' house and she came and tried to console me. I was totally devastated. I could not believe it. My dad in hospice. Not my father. Kathy helped me book a next day flight even though I already had an anticipated flight that was to leave on Saturday, the day before Fathers' Day. When I got to my dad's bedside I was so heartbroken to see him. I just started rubbing his feet and talking to him. At this point he was still able to recognize my voice and know that I was there with him. He could not speak, nor could he no longer see. That night I slept in the room with him and he seem to have slept peacefully. The next night, Friday, my dad was in so much pain. I did not sleep for watching him and feeling helpless because I could not do anything to ease his pain. This day the hospice nurse came in and provided my dad with medication for his pain. Once the medication was in his system he was resting better. He was also given oxygen and that night he was resting better than the night before. Every night I would sit and hold my dad's hand and talk to him and tell him how much I love him. I would also play his favorite gospel music.

Friday evening his pastor came and visited with him and prayed over him. I did not really want people to see my dad like that but I knew how much he loved his church family. The next day, Saturday, the 12th of June, one of his nephews and his family came and visited that evening. Around 9:30 pm his nephew left but I stayed in the room and talked to my dad. I was telling my dad that I know he is tired and I know he is in a lot of pain. I told him I did not want him in anymore pain. I told him that mom and I will be fine. I told him he raised me well and he did not have to worry about me. I told him that I was going to miss him so much but I understood if he had to leave me. At 9:40 pm I left my dad and went in the kitchen to get something to eat. As soon as I sat down I heard my dad take a deep breath which I never heard like that before. I went back in the room and I saw that my dad was not breathing. My mom came in and I just looked at her and said dad is not breathing. My mom called the hospice nurse. After she contacted the nurse she called the funeral home. While my mom was on the phone I saw my dad take two more breathes. At that time, I thought he was still with me. In my mind and heart, I felt that the last two breathes were his soul leaving his body and it was final. I just held my dad's hand and kissed his head and said I will miss you daddy. My dad was gone at 9:50 pm.

My heart was so broken. The hospice nurse came and pronounced my dad deceased and shortly afterwards the funeral home arrived. I had to watch them bring a gurney in, put my dad in a body bag, take him out of the house and put him in the back of a van. My dad was really gone and I could not do anything about it. I felt my life was over. I was so mad at God. I felt I had lost my faith. But I had to realize that they did not take my dad, they took a body that he was using. My dad was the man who taught me how to drive a stick shift. He was the man who would take me to Dairy Queen as a child. He was the man who showed me how to change my oil in my car. He was the man who took me to open my first bank account. So, I could not be upset with God for giving me a great man like my dad. I knew I had a battle of emotions to go through but I had my dad in my life for 54 years and I could not allow myself to be upset at anyone. At least for that moment. I knew it was going to be a struggle for me to get use to him not being here with me but I keep all my memories that we made together alive. Do I shed daily tears? Of course, but after shedding those tears I would try to remember a memory we shared which would make me happy. I had that many memories that would stop my tears but my life has totally changed since my dad is no longer with me. Birthdays won't be the same. Holidays won't be the same. Father's Day won't be the same. If I could have him back I would but that would be selfish of me. You never want to see a family member in pain. I have to rely on my memories of him to ease my pain while parts of me remain emotionally silent when I think about him.

CHAPTER 19

Mr. Chico

I adopted Chico after my therapist suggested that I get another dog. For the next six months we were getting to know each other. I looked forward to getting home to him after work and he was looking forward to me coming home. He was constantly following me in the house. If I was in the bathroom he would wait by the door. I would never lock him out of any room because I did not want him to feel like I was leaving him. We had a daily routine. Depending on the shift I was working, we would go for a walk before and after I got off. He was house trained so he never left me a mess to clean up. I also noticed he loved riding in a car and sitting in my lap while I drive. Chico was my therapy dog and my puppy son. Some people may not understand a puppy parent but we are very protective of our pets. When Chico and I moved to Maryland I tried to watch him very carefully around the house because I did not want him to have an accident in Kathy's house. Unfortunately, he did have a few accidents. I think some of them were accidents and some of them were because he was upset.

Kathy was not use to having a dog in her home so I was glad she welcomed Chico. I can remember Chico giving Kathy a scare. One day I went out of the garage and Chico ran behind me and ran down the street. I ran back in to tell Kathy that Chico got loose and she rushed out of her office to go outside and look for him. By the time we both got back outside, Chico was coming up the street back toward the house. That moment scared the both of us. Another funny moment happened when I was away from home. Chico was a normal boy dog and boy dogs do some strange things. I think this day Chico got a little excited and his private part was kind of poking out. Kathy thought he had hurt himself and she got nervous and did not know what to do. I explained things to her and we laughed about it later.

At the time we did not have a fenced in back yard so sometimes we would take Chico to a doggy park and let him play with other doggies. Kathy was always nervous to let him play with other dogs. She was very protective about Chico. Chico had actually become her dog. Chico had her wrapped around his finger. He knew who to go to for snacks and that was not me. I can honestly say that Kathy spoiled Chico rotten.

Once we moved on the military base we were able to have a fenced in back yard where he could play. We also had that wonderful view of the Potomac and we would take him for daily walks along the water. He loved his walks. He loved to bark at other people and other dogs. One thing I could not figure out is why Chico barked at some but not others.

Chico had his own room at the back of the house. This is how he knew when we were home because he could look out the window and see when we would pull into the garage. Once he saw us pull up he started barking as if he was reprimanding us for being gone so long. He would also sit in the window barking at people when they walked by. I must say that everyone in the neighborhood knew Chico.

For the next few years Chico was pretty much a healthy dog. He had a few dental issues but nothing major. When I adopted him the humane society said he was about 2 years old. As he got older he started having more medical issues. Around 2020 he started having issues with his kidneys. I did not realize how bad it was until the veterinarian said that he was in the early stages of kidney failure. I did not want to deal with that news but as it got worse he was having a lot of emergency visits. It really got bad during the time of my dad's illness so I was dealing with his illness as well. The month I loss my dad was the month that Chico got worse. I also knew that Kathy was dealing with his illness by herself because I was constantly trying to be by my dad's side. I really hated the fact that I could not be with her during this time. One month after the passing of my dad, we loss our Chico. Just as I witness my dad's last breath, Kathy and I had to witness Chico,s last breath. We had no choice because we did not want him to suffer in anyway. Kathy and I were very devastated. Chico was like Kathy's child. She loved him so much. She said that he brought something special to her life. We chose to cremate Chico and put him in his room. We will miss our fur baby but we know he has crossed Rainbow Bridge.

CHAPTER 20

Mental Health

There are several reasons why individuals are afraid to accept treatment for a mental illness. Some people feel ashamed because of the negative stigma of seeking out mental health intervention. Some fear the thought of being called "crazy" and the affect it would have on their careers. Many individuals don't want to admit that something is not quite right with their mental health. Trust is also something an individual fears because they don't feel comfortable sharing their personal thoughts with a stranger. Individuals also think that therapy will not help their situation. I am here to tell you that I had all of those fears but I found out it was alright to seek professional help and treatment.

Mental health is integral to total wellness and your peace of mind. People can walk around and function as if they don't have a care in the world. My mental health was tested when I was molested but was too young to know the affects it would have on my mental stability. It was tested when I was raped but I did not know the affects it would have on my lifestyle. I even saw my P.T.S.D. play a big part in my mental health because of my anger issues. It took me to a place where some days I would be totally numb. I would go to work and people would have no clue what I was going through mentally inside my head. I did not want to do anything that use to be enjoyable to me. I just wanted to sit in the dark, listen to very sad music, drink alcohol and sleep. Some days I did not even want to eat. Not being able to communicate also affected my mental health as well. I would become withdrawn and retreat from the conversations that I did not feel comfortable about. I was always able to communicate on my job only because I had to in order to make a living but when it came to personal communication it was very hard for me. I think if I was able to set boundaries in my adult life then I would not have gone through certain situations.

After being in a relationship with Kathy, I learned a lot about myself even without my therapy. I think I needed someone like her to help me understand the type of person that I was. We kind of helped each other understand ourselves. Do I get depressed sometimes, of course but not for the same reasons. Recently I have been able to start my therapy sessions again. I felt that I needed it for the sake of my mental health. I also needed it to adjust to the things I had learned about myself through Kathy. So, after 10 years I was able to locate and continue my sessions with my original therapist. She was the first person I was able to talk to and share my "emotionally silent" issues with. She was the only professional that I trusted with my feelings. Once you find that trust, then you to will be able to get through sharing anything. I am at a place where I don't worry about my mental health as much because of the people God has placed in my life. Is there a possibility for a setback, yes but I think I have a better control of things because I am able to set boundaries in my life and for my life.

Your life is your responsibility. You have the capability to choose how you want to live. It may take steps and it may be a long process but you can do it. Your life can be great if you allow it to be and you don't ever have to live "emotionally silent". Be the best "you" that you can be.

For the people who are afraid of the stigma of seeking mental health intervention, don't' be embarrassed or ashamed to ask for help. I found out that it is ok to ask and receive mental health therapy.

Final Thoughts

Through my eyes I have been through some things that only I saw.

Through my eyes I had envisioned more mother daughter moments when I was younger.

Through my eyes I have felt like I was not a good enough daughter.

Through my eyes I was always searching for love but not learning to love myself first.

Through my eyes I felt like I was not a good mate.

Through my eyes I had always tried to buy peoples love.

Through my eyes I always went from relationship to relationship and hurting people in the process.

Through my eyes it was my fault that I was molested and raped.

Through my eyes I have always tried to make sure everyone around me was happy even at the expense of me not being happy.

It took me a while to figure out what was going on in my mind and how to deal with things. How I got through everything was having positive supportive people in my circle. I also attributed going through therapy. It allowed me to release every emotion I had bottled up inside of me. It allowed me to shed tears that I had held inside for so long. I was holding those tears for fear that people would not understand the meaning of my tears. I found out that I was not at fault with any of my situations in my life.

Being "emotionally silent" held me in captivity from my freedom. What I found out was that it is not healthy to be "emotionally silent". I had finally decided that it was time for me to speak out, share my story and try to help others speak out.

Your life can be great if you allow it to be. In order to do that you must not be "emotionally silent"

Special Dedication

I want to thank a special friend (Aurelia Twitty) for being that listening ear for me during a rough time in my life. We may not have known each other long but you impacted me in a way that you understood what I was going through. Your last words to me will forever be in my heart:

Sam, I wish I could hug you! I am so happy that you came to talk to us! If you ever want to talk, feel free to call me. I am 100% in your corner. I know it may be difficult but you can do it. Remember that small steps are still steps. You got this and I'm here if you need anything.
Aurelia Twitty

Rest Well My Friend

*I want to especially thank my parents for
without them I would not be here.*

*I want to thank my family for being a
blessing to me and always having my back.*

*I want to thank all the people who have
been by my side throughout the years
during my roughest times.*

*I want to thank the people who saw
something in me that I did not see in
myself.*

*I want to thank all the people who allowed
me to stop being emotionally silent.*

*I want to especially thank a woman who
has been there for me, a woman who has
held me down, a woman who showed me
unconditional love, a woman who wiped away
my tears, a woman who supported me even
when I did not support myself, a woman who
guided me spiritually, a woman who made
me part of her family, a woman who knew
my strength when I only knew my weakness,
a woman who never gave up on me even in
the midst of our issues, a woman who put my
ambitions first before her own, a woman who
showed me what true love is.*

*I want to especially thank my wife Kathy for
being my rock. I love you more than I can
show and more than you will ever know.*

Thank You.

About the Author

Samgrelletta Fairley is a United States Air Force veteran. After separating with an Honorable Discharge, she chose a career in law enforcement and became a police officer for the next 20 years. She obtained a Bachelor's Degree in Criminal Justice with a minor in Homeland Security from the University of Maryland University College. She is currently a Personnel Security Specialist with the federal government and she resides in Washington, DC with her wife, Kathy.

When she is not writing, she enjoys cooking, bowling, taking walks near water, traveling and spending time with family. She is a sports fan and her favorite teams are Alabama Crimson Tide football, Seattle Seahawks and South Carolina Women Basketball.